Life in the Hollywood Lane

Life in the Hollywood Lane

Ann Crawford

For permission to quote brief passages, please contact
info@lightscapespublishing.com.

ISBN 978-1-948543-41-5
CIP data will be available.

Published by Lightscapes Publishing

Cover Design and Distribution by Bublish, Inc.

for

Sherry

CHAPTER 1

Act 1, Scene 1—Intro

Ever have one of those lifetimes? Yeah, me, too. This has definitely been one of 'em.

Ohhhhhhhh! (Add to that a shaking of the head and, oh, sure, even a stomping of the feet for good measure.) Wasn't there supposed to be something in particular I was supposed to be doing this particular day, this particular week, this particular month, this particular year, this particular life? Whatever it was, I'd lost track of it.

I'd lost track of it, kind of...that is, until she died. Then everything stopped swirling and settled at the bottom of the snowglobe that was my life. Slowly, over a year or so, it all became crystal clear.

Hi. Can we talk? Actually, can I just babble to you? That's kind of what I do, babble and ramble—but it's a good kind of babbling and rambling, I promise. Thanks.

My name is Trish. I'm lucky enough to call myself an actor and actually be able to name some big movies when new introductions inevitably ask, "Would I have seen you in anything?" My BFF—the bestest of bestest friends in the history of bestest, practically my sister—killed herself. I didn't write this as a downer, though...in fact, quite the opposite. Hollywood is one of the toughest towns to be successful in. It's crazy here. But, then, so am I. This wild place and I are a great match, then.

In addition to telling you a story, I want to share what life is like here—the good, the bad, the fun, the not-so-pretty. It's more of a dramedy, a look at how lovably wacky we humans are.

When I was thinking about what to call my little tale here, I thought of *The Valley of the Happy People—Not!* But I didn't want to have a big, fat negative on the cover that literally represents my life.

A screenwriting professor once told the class I attended, "You can't have a story called *The Valley of the Happy People*. No one would watch a movie where all the characters get along and are oh-so-happy-and-perfect. A story is drama, and drama needs conflict to show contrast. Characters need to grow—they have to start out one way, go through the hero's journey, and come out transformed."

In other words, screenplays are just like this life we have here. Well, hopefully….as in hopefully we come out transformed. Unless we die first. But then that's transformation, too.

I guess we can't get it wrong, really. (I'm not talking to murderers and rapists, etc. here—they get it wrong.)

Backstory

Every movie has a backstory, as they call it in "the industry"—as if there's only one industry. They call LA "the coast," too, as if there's only one coast. Interesting. Anyway, here's the backstory for my particular movie, my life.

You know the first line from *A Tale of Two Cities*? "They were the best of times, they were the worst of times." Maybe that was most people's childhoods, because that's what life is, a juxtaposition of tragedy and greatness, heartbreak and heartsongs. Funny—that's what movies are….a juxtaposition of scenes that tell a story, full of tragedy and greatness, heartbreak and heartsongs. Wow...can you imagine how much more dramatic our lives would be if we could slow down the action and add dramatic music and the odd long, meaningful glance or two?

Oh, sorry. Back to my childhood. Okay, while it was nowhere near as awful as the French Revolution must've been, it was the best and the worst of times on a less dramatic level. No one on my quiet street was sent to a guillotine, but my early years did involve sickness and death and then more sickness. I have two brothers, and my younger brother was born with a neurological condition. Instead of watching him grow up, we had to watch him grow sicker and sicker, disintegrating before our eyes. I still say I *have* two brothers because he's still my brother, at least in my heart if not in the world.

I was young when he died, so for most of my life I figured I was too young to really get it. Yeah....nice try. We get it—whatever "it" is that's happening around us—from conception. But life is also made up of everything in between the great moments and the tragedies, too. My childhood also had a lot of *ish*: strange-ish, tough-ish, okay-ish. Maybe a little this, maybe a little that.

I grew up in the middle of the Midwest, the middle child in a middle-class family. All right, Wisconsin is in the upper Midwest, but still—the middle. We're near the middle of the North American continent, so that's pretty middle. That was me: right smack dab in the middle of the middle. Even my grades were in the middle, at least they were through middle school. I was the middle one picked for teams in gym class. I suppose if I'd put a little oomph into anything, I would've been higher than the middle. But I didn't....I didn't discover the power of oomph until I got so ugly that oomph was the only thing that would save me.

My family was Catholic in a land of Lutherans—at least in my little corner of the world. Catholics make up a pretty high percentage of Wisconsinites who consider themselves religious, along with Lutherans, but we were surrounded just by Lutherans for some reason...Large Lutherans, at that. I don't mean fat, necessarily—they were tall, too. Wisconsin is one of the most German-American states in the country. But we had the messy Irish home in the midst of these tidy Germans. Ugh.

My parents could've posed for American Gothic—you know, that painting of the farmer with the pitchfork and a woman who looks to be his wife? Actually, it turns out she might be his daughter. Regardless, my mother had an uncanny resemblance to her, but airbrushed with a slight semblance of refinement. My father, who started the marriage-and-family thing late in his life, was even more dour than that farmer...now that's dour! My older brother was a younger rendition of the two of them combined. My younger brother was a cutie pie. I often wonder what he would've looked like, and sometimes when I'd spot a teenager or young man at the age he would've been with the looks he might've had, I impulsively wanted to hug the stranger.

My best friend was Jenni—complete with the circle over the i. We couldn't stand each other. I hear you, and yes, you're right, I probably shouldn't have been friends with her. It was a small town, though. There weren't too many friends to be had. What was even worse was she was BFFs with Cheryl, too, and they would make endless fun of me. I didn't realize then that that was the only thing they had in common. If they didn't have me to make fun of, they would've had nothing else to talk about—or so they might've thought. Oh, sure, everyone needs a hobby.

To be fair, I gave them some great ammunition. I had this crazy red hair that was... So. Curly. Remember Frieda from Charlie Brown, the one with the naturally curly hair? Mine was Frieda's on steroids and then put into a light socket. We didn't know where it came from—the curly part, anyway.

Throughout my childhood, especially when I was with the rest of my brown-haired family, people would ask, "Where did you get your red hair?" What a crazy question!

"From both of her grandmothers," my mother would answer.

"From my head," I started to answer when my mother was out of earshot.

And we haven't even mentioned freckles yet. I had so many that one night at a sleepover, when my buddies tried to count how many I had in one square inch, they gave up after a hundred. They played connect the dots instead. I traveled through Viet Nam once, and people would rub my arm—to see if those freaky freckles were lumpy, I guess. I asked a Vietnamese friend how I could call freckles "kisses from the sun." He told me that unfortunately the poetry would be lost in the translation. Oh, well.

How do Emma Stone and Jessica Chastain have my coloring and not have any freckles? I beat them in the thick, wavy hair department, though. Yeah, and they're crying all the way to the bank. *Bitches*.

I'm sorry. They are so not. I've met people who've worked with them, and rumor has it they're very kind. I'm just jealous. Okay—I hear you: maybe if I stop being that way I'll get ahead faster.

This was before spray tans came in to being. Now it's a non-issue. If I have to show skin and be tan(ish), I can be. And because I've stayed out of the sun, every boyfriend and massage therapist raves, "You have the best skin!"

Speaking of massage therapists, one time a friend sent me to see an energy worker. As I climbed on to her healing table, she said, "This goddess has alabaster skin, like the goddesses of the northern-European island countries." I burst into tears. First of all, I was brand new to people talking like that. Second, thinking of my alabaster skin as something beautiful or myself as anything remotely goddess-like, no matter how many people told me how beautiful I was, was light-years away from my psyche. At least it was light-years away then. That's when I started growing into myself.

But not back in Wisconsin in my early-to-middle teen years. I was fugly. This is something I wasn't in the middle of—I was at the far end of the spectrum. I would've won the frat-house dog party if I was a little older. The upside was that's when and why I got funny and smart. I frumbled (that's frumpy bumbling, my invention) through life as best I could, but I also read every book I could get my hands on and watched every movie I could find.

And then......seventeen happened. I learned how to tame my curls with a flatiron. I grew into my teeth and feet. My figure figured itself out. I learned how to use makeup to transform myself into...pretty. By the time I was nineteen, I was so crazy beautiful (thank you, makeup) that even my mother was ready to buy me a ticket to Hollywood. And she did.

When I left for California, I left all my memories and mementos behind, wanting a fresh start. But Fugly definitely came along for the ride. She's never far from me...actually, I'm thankful for that.

☆

I want to translate a few things here and there, BTW—not for you supercool cats reading this now, but for the peeps reading this thirty years from now who might say, "What the flock is she talking about?"

I don't know if Americans will still be doing the "So" thing in thirty years, but we're definitely doing it now. We start every answer, whether spoken or by email, with "So...." Even articulate, trained radio announcers and interviewees do it. I'm talking about well-polished pro-fessorial types—the younger ones, anyway. It came out of nowhere and was suddenly *everywhere.*   Another thing that's really popular now is writing in incomplete sentences. I think it should be pepper, not salt, but no one's asking me, so they're out there as massive amounts of salt. As in, massive. (Oops...there I go myself after dissing it—hehe.)

Scene 2—An Airplane Lands at LAX

That famous airport scene at the end of *Casablanca* is none other than LAX, back in the quieter day, with an outline of a minaret-y-looking structure over the shot. Didn't you think it really was in Morocco? Okay, maybe that was just me.

You know how when Dorothy lands in Oz, the movie goes from black and white to full color? That's how it was for me—even though I landed at LAX with literally a hundred bucks in my pocket. Those more awful moments of life sound so romantic in retrospect, sometimes.

Life suddenly.....bloomed—in full technicolor. Hollywood! Palm trees thrill me. The air sparkles here; I've never seen anything like it anywhere else, and by now I've been a lot of places. Those Art Deco buildings on Wilshire Boulevard hearkening back to the Golden Age of Hollywood make me feel all warm and fuzzy inside. The 'fifties-style diners with the waitresses, seemingly still from that era, feel like home. The Hollywood sign lifts my spirits even on the downest of days.

The whole town is even more beautiful at night. The streetlights have a golden glow that lights up those palm trees, and of course when you're up in the hills, the vista of the Hollywood lights is pure exhilarating enchantment.

We'd taken a family trip to Disneyland when I was eight and my older brother was ten. Six-year-old Brian was in a wheelchair already. That was the first time we kids saw the ocean; the smell, the sparkling air, and waves lapping around my feet was practically a mystical experience for me. Years later, Kevin just remembered massive amounts of traffic and hating that Goofy laughed at him. I remembered palm trees and that mighty ocean as well as Minnie Mouse and Sleeping Beauty loving on my "oh-so beautiful hair." They fussed and fussed and fussed over it.

That might've been the last time we were happy as a family, because Brian suddenly became even sicker and died not long after that. But for just a while, we were so very happy together, experiencing the captivating charm of Disneyland and Southern California.

The magic of that trip has stayed with me. Still, to this day, when I stick my feet in the sand, they tingle for a week. That didn't happen in my backyard.

Speaking of traffic, most people's first question might be, "What about the traffic?" What traffic? I don't do traffic. I never have to be out in the morning rush hour, and I arrive where I need to be before the evening rush hour, even if I have to hang out in a café for a while.

We talk about traffic like it's a living, breathing thing. And it is. It's like a person we get to blame—"Oh, I can't make it because of the traffic." "Oh, I would've been here earlier but the traffic." That *Saturday Night Live* comedy skit about the Californians had just about every conversation involve how we drive here. "Oh, I took the 405 to the 10 to La Brea...." It's true! We do talk like that here.

But even when I drove around shedding tears while playing the love-song channel, feeling a tug on my heart as I listened to dedications from people who'd been married for thirty years, every day was a thrill. (This was before I knew to be *happy* for them, not resentful. Actually, I wasn't resentful, just wistful. But wistful is not a powerful rocket booster for creating, either.) My heart expanded at every palm tree. That's a lot of expanding! There was no place on Earth I'd rather have been. Sometimes I was miserable. Sometimes I was ecstatic. Sometimes I was both in the very same moment.

When I moved to Hollywood, I had to take informal elocution lessons to turn my long Wisconsin vowels into the shorter vowels of the transcontinental accent. Sooooo had to become so. Wiscaaaaaaaaaaaansin had to become Wisconsin. We're not quite as long as what you heard in *Fargo* or *New in Town* (that great flick with Renée Zellweger), doonchoou knooow, but we're close. Noootice I said "long" instead of "bad." Accents aren't bad—they make things more interesting. Imagine if the whole country spoke the same way. For one thing, *Fargo* wouldn't have been nearly so funny. But you can get more acting gigs when you can *do* an accent, not *have* an accent.

A lot of folks around here talk in a happy whine. And even if it's happy, it's still a whine. And it has a lot of h's. "Hihhhhhh. Howhh hhaarrrre hyohhhhhuh? Hohhhhh, whhhhat a ghorgheous neckhhhhhlace."

Being from solid, no-nonsense Midwestern stock, I found it hard to whine. When I really had the urge, I had Cyn to whine to....but ours was high-level, existential whining. Of course.

My Costar

Cyn. Oh, Cyn. We met just a month or so after I arrived here—we were both auditioning for the same commercial. Cyndi was my age, my height, my temperament, my tempo. She had red hair, too, but hers was long, luxurious, and straight. Plus, she was relieved of those pesky freckles. (Speaking of that commercial audition, it was my first; Cyn wasn't the only one in the room who was my age and size with red hair; it was the oddest feeling to be in a room of women who could've been near clones.)

We became instaBFFs and eventually roomies. A native Los Angeleno (there are a few), she showed me around town—all the hip nightclubs, where the cutest guys hung out, the cool thrift stores, the private beach spots...everything.

Cyndi had always been beautiful. She didn't have to become funny and smart (although she was both in spades) to compensate for any lack whatsoever. She lacked nothing, absolutely nothing, at least as far as the eyes could see. At times she could've been the instigation for the term *hot mess*. Most of the time she kind of... drooped. I don't mean in a bad posture kind of way—she drooped in that she was so warm, so loving, so oozy. Maybe I mean dripped, not drooped. She just kind of melted alllllll over the place. She dripped so much that people would run after her with dustpans and saucepots to catch this particular saucepot's spillage, lap her up, try to dive in to the puddles she left behind to perhaps have some of her magic rub off on them. Picture a modern-day Marilyn Monroe but less ditzy, with more substance and just as much glamour and ooh la la.

As an aside, I'm sure Norma Jean wasn't ditzy at all and had a ton of substance. She'd have to have had (wow, is that a clunky sentence or what?) a lot of substance to carry the persona of Marilyn.

Men and women young and old, kids, pets, even garden gnomes, I bet, found Cyn irresistible. I swear our houseplants brightened when she walked by, and they would've followed her around the house if they could've. Same with the garden gnomes—those rascals!

Lots and lots of folks asked if we were sisters. Not only did we look alike, we also moved alike, dressed alike, talked alike (after those elocution lessons sunk in). We went to the same hairstylist and shopped in the same stores. But no one was running after me with saucepans.

She was soooooo easygoing, too. She rarely got ruffled—a drama queen with a penchant for the macabre at times, yes, but that was more for fun and show, or so I thought. I wished she'd become more ruffled and stuck around more. I get ruffled, unfortunately. I.....worry. What, me worry? Yes, all the time. As in...ALL the time. It gives me something to do so maybe I won't HAVE to worry so much. It's as though I might forestall the need for worrying if I outworry the worry. If I worry a lot, I might have less to worry about, the less I'd *need* to worry...kind of like I'm pre-empting it. Does that make any sense at all? Probably not—but it did to me.

One time a couple of friends were discussing something that might not go well. One said, "Don't worry. Trish will worry about it for you." Meanwhile, I was on the other side of town, nowhere near this conversation! Ack.

I'll fill you in more on Cyn as we go along. For right now, hmmmmm...what else can I tell you? We loved it there. But, like most everyone else there, we were slightly, well, malcontent. You never fully arrive at your destination here. It's never a job well done—at least not for more than five minutes.

My dad was a dreamer guitar and piano player— meaning he dreamed about it more than he played them, and never actually put together a band or searched out gigs. But he did have a subscription to *Rolling Stone*. When I was way too young to grok that magazine but read it anyway, ridiculously precocious kid that I was, I read an article in which Carrie Fisher interviewed Madonna. Now there were two women near the top of their games. I think Carrie asked Madonna something along the lines of, "Do you ever feel like you've made it?"

"Not in this town," or something very close to that, was Madonna's response.

We'd been working this gig for twenty years. Still nothing—nothing major, anyway. Cyn and I got a little lucky, I guess. By the time we were in our mid-thirties, we'd both had enough low-level success to at least pay the basics—food, rent, gym membership, weekly massage. (Hey, *you* try to make it in this town! I chose that luxury over almost everything else.) I'd been cast as the lead's sister in some zombie flick that became a cult classic that played over and over and over again. If you're ever up late and you see early-twenty-something zombies from a couple of decades ago, you'll see me. Cyn had been in enough commercials to keep her fed, well-coiffed, and beautifully dressed. She was also in a number of print ads, which she loved because she didn't have to wake up before the birds to get to set; print photographers want those models looking well-rested, since it's a still shot. Those early mornings don't show on the face as much in moving pictures.

But it wasn't enough....maybe for the checkbook somewhat...but not for the soul. Nothing was really wrong; it was just some mucky malaise that felt like every day was something to slog through. I've heard it said that having dreams to pursue makes life interesting. But having them *not* come true, year after year, can make life a slogfest...emphasis on slog and none on fest.

Relative to some people in some places, it could be viewed as close to perfect. Except it wasn't. I could live the charade, even have many, many moments of bliss. I had my palm trees, the Hollywood sign, and near-perfect weather all year, plus I had Cyndi and the cats.

Someone once suggested to me not to put any part of life on hold while I was waiting for career and marriage and family and all that to happen. Cyn and I did not have our lives on hold. But they were so *not* on hold that they didn't let anyone else fit in, really.

And so the years passed...suddenly forty was on the near horizon. How'd that happen? Cyndi's malcontent turned into misery. She was a few months younger, and she warned me she wouldn't take kindly to forty. She was always being dramatic. How could I have known that this was the time to pay more attention?

Forty came and went for me, but not for her. She killed herself the night before her fortieth birthday.

CHAPTER 2

Love in a Jar

Was I staring at the almost-empty jar of peanut butter,
or was it staring back at me? *Organic*, the label
announced. What words could be made from the word
organic? Nag. Rag. Rig. Okay, those were too easy; I
switched to four letters. Gain. Rain. Narc. Rang.

Carrie Fisher wrote about eating peanut butter in bed
in *Postcards from the Edge*....which was about a famous
actor who made it really big on one movie. (One recommended rule of writing is to write about what you know.)
I love how she turned her autobiography into a comedy.
In the book, she'd sit in bed eating peanut butter. There's
a good reason for that—it's the *ultimate* comfort food.

The yapper dogs next door started their daily yapping.
Ugh! We had neighbors with a screaming toddler, plus
the dad played the tuba. Frequently. Cyn and I would
long for them to leave. We were so happy when we saw a
moving truck pull up in front of their house one day. That
one darling, adorable, fabulous, screaming toddler and
that dear, old, tuba-aficionado dad was replaced with
four screaming kids, three yapper dogs, two smokers...
and perhaps a partridge in a pear tree. Who the hell
smokes anymore, anyway? I'll take that tuba back!

On my moving-in day, the tuba blared.

"I've been meaning to tell you about the whale that
lives next door," Cyn chuckled.

Cyn. Oh, Cyn. You were so funny, so silly, so much
fun, so outrageous, so out there. Now you're really out
there. You were so...strong, so...amazing, so...alive. So...
much for that.

I couldn't even cry, I was so numb. I couldn't move,
couldn't eat, couldn't get out of bed, could barely muster
the strength to go to the bathroom, which didn't happen

all that much because I wasn't drinking or eating any-thing at all, other than the odd spoonful of peanut butter. My body started aching from the lack of movement, but I ignored it.

Cyndi. Why? Whywhywhywhywhywhywhywhy?

Sweetie, I said inside my head to her when the numb-ness stopped for a minute, if I knew that in your heart of hearts you really wanted to do this, I would've held your hand as you went out. Okay, maybe not. I would've held your hand and called 911. You probably knew that.

You were more than my best friend. You were my sis-ter by another mister. You were the love of my life, even though it was never a romantic or sexual thing. I didn't know this until you left me.

Mom flew out to tend to me. Normally having her around wouldn't be viewed as a favor, but this time it was. She stayed on her "best behavior," fortunately....I'll explain more about that later. She dealt with Cyndi's parents because I couldn't—I couldn't answer their questions or deal with the utter heartbreak in their eyes that I knew would be there, and I would be grilled: Why didn't you tell us? Why didn't you know? We trusted you! How could you let us down like this? Why didn't you save her?

I didn't know she was so close to the edge. And if I had known, I still wouldn't have known....that there was nothing I could do and nothing I could say, that it wasn't even my responsibility. But right then, I wasn't thinking any of that. I was thinking that I should have known, that I should have said something, that it was completely my responsibility. And if I hadn't failed so miserably at said responsibility, Cyndi would still be here, dramati-cally brooding over her morning coffee, laughing at my jokes, making me laugh at her jokes, teasing the house-plants with her ooziness, coming up with some crazy shenanigan or another.

It's completely my fault.

Somewhere in the far recesses of my mind, I knew that was a crock, but right then that thought reigned front and center.

It was this town, wasn't it, Cyn? This fucking town—it can chew you up and spit you out like no other. It was acting, too, wasn't it? This fucking career—it, too, can chew you up and spit you out like no other.

She'd met someone just a few weeks beforehand. Oh, Cyn. How many times did I suggest that you just tell potential beaus everything (well, perhaps not *everything*) up front so they're not surprised. He was from Europe and was so taken by her beauty, her carriage, her demeanor. He thought she was a real movie star. But by their third or fourth date, she let him know that she was a star of a number of commercials, but not much more than that. He left—the cad.

"Crazy fucking town. Crazy fucking people. Crazy fucking everything about this place." Even the successful ones, as I mentioned earlier, say they never feel like they've arrived. "Perhaps if we would've arrived without it," I said to the air.

Hah! That's the whole secret of life, isn't it? Be happy with what is. We all know that, somewhere deep inside in there. But there can be a long journey between *knowing* the secret and truly *being* happy.

We talked about the elusiveness of high-level success all the time.

"It's right near me," Cyn said once, "but it's just out of reach. It's floating in my periphery."

Most of our myriad esoteric conversations took place in our two persimmon-colored overstuffed, scrumfy (scrumptiously comfy, my invention) chairs, with morning coffee or evening wine sitting nearby on the huge slab of oak that served as our coffee table. An equally overstuffed, comfy sofa sat on the other side of the table, beckoning everyone who saw it to stretch out and forget the problems of the world. A petite person could nearly disappear in our furniture. Our beds were super scrumfy, too.

Oh, I haven't told you about our darling, little hobbit house yet! It was absolutely adorable. Tucked away in a grove of trees in the hills of Glendale, you could easily see Frodo walking in to this part cottage, part living fairy tale. It was painted the cheeriest yellow you could stand without being nauseated, and it had rounded recesses over the rounded, latticed windows. Even the top of the door was rounded.

And......it came with fairly low rent! Cyndi's mom was in real estate and owned a ton of rental properties. She let her daughter live in this one for a song, and Cyn had a ragtag bunch of odd roommates until I moved in. (Maybe I could be counted as ragtag and odd, too, though?)

Colorful artwork from our multitude of colorful artist friends lined the butter-yellow walls. Little palm trees were tucked into every nook and cranny, and this little hobbit house had plenty of those.

There was no carport, but that's okay. In the whole time I've been in LA, I've had to scrape ice off my windshield twice.

We even had a bit of a view from the deck, since we were up a hill a bit. We couldn't see the ocean, but on a clear day we could see that far out, so I'd imagine I was looking at it. At night we saw lights; it wasn't anything like the Hollywood lights, but I liked to pretend it was a snippet of them, instead of just downtown Glendale.

Anyway....(Don't you hate it when people say that? I do, so I take it back!) Here's one version of our many conversations regarding success (or lack thereof) where one of us would play devil's advocate to exorcise our holding-back demons.

"Why don't you want to be an actor?"

"I do!"

"No, you don't."

"Yes, I do. There's nothing I want more than to be an actor. Acting and movies help people open their hearts and give them something to think about that they wouldn't have thought about otherwise. It's my calling. It's what I want to do. It's in my soul."

"You'd be there if you really wanted to be."

"I want to be!"

"No, you don't."

"Yes, I do."

"No, you don't. Otherwise you'd be there."

That conversation happened on many occasions, with each of us taking a turn on each side. Sometimes it helped. Here's another one, which had taken place just a few weeks before she died:

"What'd make it come in for a landing?" I asked her referring to the ever-elusive, circling success, while asking myself at the same time.

"Dunno. Right timing? A better me?"

"Nah. There couldn't be a better you." I was in one of those moods—beneficent, which might've annoyed the bejesus out of her if she hadn't been slightly tipsy already. "You're the best you you are. Besides, it's not about deserving. Nasty, abusive drunks make it big all the time."

She took another sip of wine. And two. And three. Wait a minute—why didn't I see this at the time?

"Invite it in," I continued. "Make it welcome. Serve it tea and crumpets."

She nearly spit out her wine. "Tea and crumpets?"

"Well, if not that, what does it want? Beer and brats? Champagne and caviar?"

The wine was starting to make itself known in her system and speech. "Maybe it's an agreement I made before I came in to this lifetime—that success will weasel away from me this time around. This one isn't my lifetime to be successful because I'm here to experience what trying and trying and trying feels like."

"I can't imagine making that kind of agreement."

"Maybe I'm just supposed to light things up no matter what I do."

"Maybe."

"What about people who never, ever find the 'one'—or the two or three if they're into that kind of thing. Some people are lonely their whole, entire lives."

"And some people are lonelier inside a sad marriage than some people are on their own. But wouldn't folks be married if they really, really wanted to be?"

"Wouldn't I be a star if I really wanted to be?"

"Maybe you don't have to be a star—be a starburst! Light up the world everywhere you go."

She downed the rest of her wine.

Maybe if I hadn't used the tea-and-crumpets metaphor, she'd still be alive.

Yes, of course I'm being facetious, but not about this....If only she hadn't taken me so literally about being a starburst.

Starve the Fever; Feed the Soul—and Stay Forever Young While We're at It

I stared at the ceiling while Mom cleaned the house. There was no point telling her we (uh, now I) had a housekeeper; she needed something to do. What about my....oh, which job did I have those days, anyway?

Jobs, jobs, jobs. I've had a few: Waitperson. Ice cream scooper. Retail. Hotel front desk. Then I realized I could take care of two things at once by being something physical. So I—oh, you name it, I did it—was a yoga teacher,

Pilates teacher, Zumba teacher, CrossFit trainer, even a personal trainer.

But being self-employed didn't really work either. I would fret so much about making a living that it was like I was stepping on my own garden hose of creativity. When I worked at a regular job, the hose would flow; because money was taken care of, I freed up the ability to express. My soul yearned to create—doing one-woman shows, taking acting classes, coming up with collaborations, writing songs and screenplays.

One thing I love about writing is that everything can be a part of writing. It's not just the times sitting in front of the computer. Doing the dishes, driving, taking a shower—those are the times the ideas really come.

I'd be expressing so much that I'd yearn for more time. So I'd think about what could give me more time? Working for myself, of course. But as soon as I'd go back in that direction, I'd be so worried about money that I'd drop all my acting classes and the cursor in the middle of that empty page on the computer screen would mock me.

Luckily, over time, the zombie money and a trickle of other royalties took the pressure of self-employment off, and I'd still pick up odd jobs and personal training here and there. So, what was it I was doing those days? I literally couldn't remember. Wasn't there somewhere I had to be? I didn't care.

Ohhh, it was helping an older hippie writer chick, who smelled of patchouli oil, with her life—personal training, organizing her house and her affairs, and then launching her social media and blog. The personal training had come first, and then as we grew closer and closer, she asked for more and more help. It's not that I was an organizing or social-media superstar, but compared to her I certainly was.

Skye was so cool. Age is an actor's worst fear, but she made seventy-five look hip and fun. She eschewed makeup, but that didn't matter—her eyes shined like beacons, and those were what people noticed. They were perhaps made even more special because they were framed by beautiful skin and thick, long, flowing, white hair. I didn't know what her secret was...I hoped that whatever it was, it'd rub off on me in the time we spent together. (I'm talking about her secret for happiness and glowing eyes, of course. Actually, she did tell me what her secret for amazing skin and thick hair was: Vitamin E, Black Currant-seed Oil, and Collagen. As soon as I left her house that day, I immediately stopped at a health-food store and bought all three.)

The week before Cyn was supposed to turn forty, I tried telling her about all the women I know who loved their forties, fifties, sixties, and especially Skye loving her seventies.

"Freedom comes with age.

"Not in this industry," she said.

"Look at Meryl, look at Jane and Lily."

"I don't want to look at them. They made it in their twenties. They can do whatever they want now."

Organ. Cargo. Grain. Still in bed with my peanut butter, at least I was up to five-letter words from *organic*. Okay, yes, organ was totally cheating.

I remembered hearing once that the brain can't really feel pain if it's entirely focused on one task. As soon as the task of word-making stopped, the pain rushed in—at least until it got to be so much that the numbness would set in again. My brain swirled with "If only I'd said..." "Perhaps if I'd...." "Maybe if I'd moved out...."

So much was starting to dawn on me. Perhaps if we hadn't lived together so long, we each might've found a solid partner—a Bogey for her Bacall, a Tracy for my

Hepburn—to make a life with. Maybe then we wouldn't have fed off of each other's misery so much.

I wasn't that miserable, was I? Not that much, really. Oh, maybe I was a bit. I was born with a sense of optimism that carried me through my bleakish childhood in Wisconsin and my years in one of the toughest towns in the world. You can't attempt this business unless you have some steel and grit and tons of patience. It does wear you down, though. Maybe I was more miserable than I knew.

Oh, Cyn—yes, it's ridiculously hard here. But we deal with life as best we can. Sometimes that means cutting our losses and making do with what we have.

"Fuck it!" That's what she said back during the conversation about older women. She probably would've said it again to what I just thought.

She cut a whole lot more than her losses.

Oh, Cyn. I'm so sorry I didn't say the right thing to make it all worthwhile to you. What could I have said? What could I have done?

A crystal hanging in the window turned slightly and suddenly sparkled in the sunshine, casting little dancing rainbows around the room. I thought back a few weeks to when I was struck by the sudden sparkle in Cyn's wineglass as she walked under the track lighting in the living room.

"The story is in the details," a filmmaking professor once said. I've taken classes in every aspect of this industry, and the ones in the actual art of filmmaking were among my favs.

In that particular student film, the shot was an ECU (extreme closeup) of the sun shining through a piece of kiwi in a child's hand. The close-up of the seeds and rays shooting out from the center of the fruit slice was a metaphor: in this case the little girl was the light in the life of the family.

A big part of Cyn's story might've been in that one detail, that one sparkle. How much did she have to drink? No......it couldn't have been that whole bottle already. And did she drink that other bottle, too? And perhaps a couple of bottles the day before? How could I not have noticed this before? I might've been a big drinker, too, especially given what this town can do to the soul, if I hadn't been so crazy calorie conscious.

How did I end up having to make all the arrangements for the place, the food, the everything?

"Her parents can't do it," Mom said. "They just can't."

"Like I can?"

"I'll do it. Just help me a little. What were her favorite foods? What were her favorite flowers? And what colors did she love best?"

That was the thing about Cyn—as miserable as she must've been, she also loved so many things. I don't think there was a food on Earth (as long as it wasn't once a bug or a reptile) she met that she didn't fall in love with. And flowers and colors? Loving one kind over another would've left the others bereft. She didn't have many favorites—she loved all of them. She loved everything. She loved life. Or so I thought.

Go Mom! She handled everything. Once I recommended some flowers and food items, she went to town— or at least to Costco. She sat at my computer for a day or two writing up the memorial and emailing my friends.

"Make sure you tell everyone to wear bright colors," I told her. "Cyndi would hate it if everyone was in black or somber stuff."

Mom went into Cyndi's closet to see what colors she wore. If there's a color, it was in Cyndi's closet. Yes, that's an exaggeration, but not much. Finally Mom figured that a coral-y/watermelon-y color seemed to show up more than any other.

"She called that color *happy*," I said, bursting into tears.

"Honey, I don't know if I should just leave you alone or make you go out or what."

"'Or what' sounds good."

"And what does 'Or what' look like?"

Well, my body was growing stiff from lying in bed for days, and Malibu would always be first on any or-what list. After nearly shoving me in the shower, Mom drove my car while I stared at a few wispy clouds. We each grabbed one of those decadent, caramel-y things at the Starbucks in the Trancas shopping center. Jane Fonda and Lily Tomlin sat in that parking lot during one episode of *Grace and Frankie*.

"Hey, that's my parking lot!" I shouted.

"A little possessive, are we?" Cyn chuckled.

Cyn. For a few seconds here and there, I'd forget about her dying, but then waves of utter sadness would wash over me.

Mom and I sipped our drinks at my favorite beach spot. After that we wandered through a few shops down the highway. I was numb; two minutes later I'd want to scream at the top of my lungs.

I'd heard that grief gets worse after the balm of the initial shock wears off. Grrrreeeaaaaat.

The Performance of a Lifetime

Cyndi greeted us at her memorial, from those big, blue eyes smiling out from my favorite picture of her, blown up to poster size. It was a perfect day—springtime really is the best time of year in LA.

There were probably a thousand people there—one of the benefits of being such a phenomenal person and then dying in your hometown. Many people stood up to lavish beautiful words on her.

"She was the brightest light I ever met, and she helped everyone around her to shine brightly, too."

"She'd walk into a room, and it was like the sun just came out."

"She'll never know this now, but she taught me to be fearless."

"...kind..."

"....forthright...."

".....amazing....."

"......incomparable....."

".......special......."

"........SO funny........"

".........beautiful inside *and* out........."

"..........a kick in the pants when I needed it.........."

"...........the life of the party as well as the party of the life..........."

"............one of my best friends............"

Who were all these people? And why don't we say these things *before* someone dies? Actually, a buddy of mine knew he was dying and had a party—a living memorial—so he could hear all the wonderful things his friends wanted to say about him. But he knew he was dying. I doubt Cyndi knew, *really* knew, until the very last few seconds.

Her mom stood up and asked, "How many of you thought you were one of Cyndi's best friends?" About half the people in the room raised a hand. We all laughed. That was so Cyn.

After the last speaker shared, I stood up and started applauding. The entire assembly stood up and started applauding, as well—giving Cyndi a standing ovation for her life. Her beautiful life. Her beautiful, too-short life. As we clapped and clapped and clapped and clapped, some started hooting, shouting, stamping, and whistling, like people do after a stunning performance.

"Cyn, can you hear all this now?" I asked her, wherever she was. "I tried to tell you." But sometimes we fade out the voice of the one who loves us the most and listen only to the voice that we've trained to pull us down.

Afterward, I wanted to call my best friend and tell her about the truly amazing memorial service I'd just witnessed. "Oh, yeah. I forgot. It was for *you.*"

I went back to bed. The palm tree outside my window didn't even gift the little lift to my heart the way it always did, no matter what, not even for a split second. Wow, that's bad.

I've got to get out of this place, I thought. Maybe I'll import sweaters from New Zealand and sell them at a little kiosk in the Mall of America. Maybe I'll grow pot in Humboldt county. Maybe I'll go can salmon in Alaska. Maybe I'll go back to Wisconsin and work in the Harley Davidson factory. (My dad took me on the tour there once when I was a kid; those guys were some kind of *happy.* Really. They left a lasting impression on me.) Maybe I'll go knit baby things in a cabin near Mendocino. I guess I'd have to learn to knit first. Minor detail. Maybe I'll....

Mom and I turned Cyn's Facebook page into a memorial page. She'd asked me a few months earlier if I'd be her Legacy Contact for Facebook if anything should happen to her. Duh! Good gravy, Trish—talk about hints. But I was rushed in that moment and even if I hadn't been, I might've thought she was just being her melodramatic yet practical self. People wrote and wrote and wrote the most beautiful things about her—like what they said at the memorial but even more moving, which I wouldn't have thought possible.

"If something only gets fifteen likes on Facebook," Cyndi once jokingly grumbled about a post that wasn't receiving the attention she thought it deserved, "did it happen? I mean, it needs at least two hundred likes to have happened, right?"

"You certainly happened, Cyn," I said out loud as the tributes grew from the hundreds into the thousands.

CHAPTER 3

Onward Ho, Right? Yeah, about That

Even the song about big, loud dreams and clouds didn't lift my spirits as I drove. I switched the radio station to something gloomier. I had a dream like that, I thought. Maybe it's time for something else.

People can't be a SAG (Screen Actors Guild) actor until they've been in some SAG movies, and they can't get into SAG movies until they've become a SAG actor. For the non-SAG to land a part in a SAG movie, actors have to know someone who can open doors. And I do.

My agent, a doppelgänger for Bette Midler in *Hello, Dolly!* (slightly smaller hats, though, but just as flamboyant and enthusiastic), is on a first-name basis with many of the casting directors. Cara can get meetings at Paramount, Universal, TriStar, everywhere. She puts us in for everything she possibly can—TV shows, movies, commercials—for twelve to fourteen hours a day, hardly even coming up for air. If we want to meet with her we have to feed her by taking her to lunch or dinner (never breakfast). She lives on peanut butter on crackers, otherwise, and happily so. When she gets paid those huge sums (not! at least not often) for getting us gigs, she lavishes it on...us. She spends it all on her flock of ducklings, as she calls us, paying for headshots, video reels, and lunch if we're between jobs.

She gives us something special that we can't get anywhere else: a touch of old Hollywood. Hundreds of old-time gadgets and gizmos and prints and paintings celebrating the Golden Hollywood Era fill her home/office. But it's not just in things that she gives the feel of old Hollywood. Some days she can look like the other Bette, although pronounced differently, as well: Bette Davis—on a good day.....well, usually, that is. She has her moments after pulling an all-nighter for us, and then she's Bette on a bad day...and I'm talking like straight out of *Hush...Hush, Sweet Charlotte* or *Whatever Happened to Baby Jane?* How could one person look like Bette and Bette? Well, Cara pulls it off somehow.

She's seen so many trends and fads and phases come and go. She was first to get on the techno-geek train, just before all the TV shows suddenly had a beautiful killer with black-rimmed glasses who can work a computer like it's a child's toy in order to take over the world. She saw that trend coming, along with many, many others.

High tech she's not. Usually some Millennial intern volunteers do her tech tasks for her like update the website and do the social-media stuff. It's usually some young softies who wanted a brush with the Hollywood dream without having to go through the heartache—live the palm tree, convertible, Malibu, *Hollywood Reporter* thing until it got boring, because they were completely missing the point, and then go back to Kentucky and Iowa.

Over the years I've helped Cara do submissions for "breakdowns," as they're called...the casting directors put out a list, a breakdown of the kind of characters they're looking for in upcoming filmings. For some cop show, for instance, they could ask for "Caucasian man, 35, drug addict" and "African American woman, 42, steely-eyed scientist." These are for acting roles, those with lines. There are other companies that handle the extras. For main TV shows, the ones with the leads already established, the roles can be very small all the way up to the main guest star. During pilot season, when the networks (and Netflix, et al.) are putting together new shows, the breakdown includes the leads. For movies, the list can go on for pages. Sometimes no age, race, or gender is mentioned, so Cara puts in most of her peeps.

Oh—the hours and dedication this woman puts in is beyond the beyond.

So...love? No agent loves her actors more. She never had kids. She'd been proposed to numerous times, but "Getting hitched and starting a family never seemed to be the right thing to do at that particular time," she'd laugh. We were her kids, and she loved us beyond the norm. I'm not sure my own mother loved me more. For some of us, this was the first motherly love we really received. (My mom tried, truly. More about that in a bit.) And it is totally reciprocated; her actors swoon over her, fuss over her, and stumble over each other to dote on her. She calls us all honey, and we all call her dear. One of the biggest surprises about LA is how often everyone calls everyone dear. It reminds me of my long-gone grandparents.

Another thing to get used to in LA is how people shower little gifties on each other all the time—even if the two people just saw each other two days ago. I'd never seen anything like it, but I quickly learned: never show up anywhere empty-handed. They also do that double-sided-air-kissing-face-to-face-touching thing like they do in Europe.

I walked into Cara's office bearing flowers for her. Even all the movie mementos and posters didn't pick up my spirits.

"Hooooonnnnnnneeeeeeey!" She flew across the room, arms outstretched, and wrapped me in her hug. No one else hugs like that. It's so wonderful to get that hug any time, but especially after a rock-solid audition, then four callbacks, and *still* not get the role. And even more especially today. We did the double-sided-air-kissy thing about fourteen times.

"Honey, how are you doing?"

She'd been at the memorial since she'd been Cyndi's agent, too, at one point, but we hadn't really talked.

"Maybe you could send me out for another zombie audition," I groaned. "It wouldn't be acting."

Earlier I mentioned that LA has 'fifties-style diners and restaurants tucked in here and there all around town. Some are kind of Art Deco, all are definitely a step back in time. They remind me of my grandmothers' living rooms. And the waitresses (I know that's politically incorrect, but these gals are still waitresses), even the young ones, definitely remind me of my grandmothers.

Canter's Deli on Fairfax is my fav, although I can't say that in mixed company. It's just not cool to a few of my oh-so-tremendously-stylish peeps (so that's more about them than Canter's), who just have to flock to the newest trendy place. But Canter's does make the LA *Hotlist* quite a bit. I love going there.

For some reason they kept the phone jacks in the booths—a throwback to the pre-cell-phone days when managers, actors, agents, and producers would tell their people where they'd be, so they could receive calls. The restaurant manager would bring the phone to the table and plug it in.

Cara prefers HMS Bounty over on Wilshire, but she acquiesced this once in honor of my broken heart. Oh, all those lunches with Cara—we'd spend so many hours dreambuilding and going over photographs and scripts and just yakking. This time I didn't feel much like yakking.

Cara took my hand. "Why don't you take a break, honey?" she suggested. "Why don't you take a trip or go home for a bit?"

Home? LA is my home. Going to my previous home grew to be a chore. People were glad to see me, but always lurking in the undergrowth of their effusive flattery was that unspoken "Haven't you made it YET?"

They had no idea. When someone shows up on a TV program or in a movie or even at an awards show, it looks so easy, so "of course." Before that day came years and years of acting classes, auditions, workouts at the gym, schmoozing at parties to meet that singular someone who knows someone who's looking for someone just like that particular actor. We have to be more than devoted. We have to be beyond obsessed.

So, why haven't I made it yet? Listen, pal—do you have any idea how much it takes to "make it"? Friends who've landed parts in soaps told me they get ridiculed "back home," but hey, it's a start, it's good money, it's something really big in our world. Also, do they have any idea how many people who make it have a parent in the industry? The kid's talent has to stand on its own, of course, but the doors open more easily to let that talent shine and be seen by the right person in the right place. Many more have relatives and friends of the family who work in a studio or with a casting director or someone else who can open the door. I miss the idea of the ice-cream parlor where Lana Turner was, rumor has it, discovered.

Over the years I've heard my actor friends talk less and less about their auditions and more and more about their construction projects, small businesses, real-estate jobs, or the little stores they've opened.

They (whoever *they* are) say that most people who come to LA to act last about three years. I heard about one young woman who came, had one audition, and went right back home to Kansas, or wherever she came from. Okay, it was Ohio. That intrigued me, and I was even a little envious that she wasn't plagued/haunted/fixated on this crazy acting thing. Obviously it wasn't her thing, and hopefully she quickly moved on to whatever her thing was. Sometimes I wish my thing was....anything else.

Some of my peeps who call themselves "actors," well, aren't...actors, that is. They show up late and/or blow their auditions—kind of on purpose. Me? I'm never late for an audition. Never. Not once. If there's ever an accident on a freeway, I take the next exit and race through backcountry surface roads. As I mentioned, I usually leave hours ahead of time anyway; if I'm early, I write or make calls. But I'm never, ever late...at least not any more. One day back in Wisconsin, I arrived at a restaurant ten minutes late and full of apologies.

"No problem," my friend said. "I expected it. Being late is part of your persona. It's who you are."

Boom! Yuck—never again would that be part of my persona. Brings tears to my nose.

As for those actors who blow their auditions, maybe they don't really want it. They want the dream. They don't want to wake up at four AM and actually put their heart and soul into something and then be out in the world wide open to massive criticism. They'd rather cater or Uber and complain that they haven't gotten their lucky break yet.

There's a book called *The Snow Leopard* where two men trek through Nepal trying to find the elusive, rarely seen (you guessed it—you're so smart!) snow leopard. Spoiler alert: they never do find the special animal. What they do find was that the search, the journey, was the destination all along.

For some it's a dream, and part of the dream is just having the dream and not necessarily living it. Sometimes having the dream is more important than living the reality...for some—not for me. I tried giving up this dream soooooo many times. It is ridiculously hard out here. But this dream seems to have me even more than I have it.

You know how magazines and newspapers have those "Where Are They Now" articles, referring to actors we haven't seen in a while? They always seem to be in real estate. In some of my less optimistic moments, I'd think well, why not try it out since I'll end up doing it eventually anyway? Or I could be a script supervisor, or a talent agent, or....anything else.

If actions speak louder than words, my actions showed me where my heart was and is. I'd start looking for jobs on Indeed.com, and suddenly my mouse would be clicking on "pay" for another acting class. I'd start working on my resume, and suddenly my mouse would be clicking on a photographer's website for more headshots.

Plus, the characters I've played would tap me on the shoulder and whisper, "I was only here because you breathed life into me."

"That's not exactly true," I'd reply. "Any other actor could've played you."

"Not the way you did."

"Then this has to be easier."

Oh, how the answer to that one would vary: "It will be. Just hang in there." "What's the point in it being easier? The struggle makes the reward that much sweeter." "You're in charge of that."

Uh, so, well, yes, I have voices in my head. They're friendly, though—it's not like they tell me to pick up a gun or anything like that. I'm not exactly sure where they come from, but I do have an extremely vivid imagination.

I'm also like a dog with a bone—I'm not going to give up until it's chewed up. I mean get the reward. It'd be so much easier to just go do something else. Well, maybe it wouldn't, because there'd always be a pang in my heart that I'd given up, and I'd always wonder what could've been. I'm going to die trying.

Cyndi died trying.

Did I Tell You…

that my mom was a drinker? I might've been saving that little tidbit of info for now. I heard through her former high-school classmates that she was always quite the wild one at parties, but she really started after my little brother died.

It might've been easier to be beaten every day. At least I would've known where I stood with her. But just about every time I saw her, even if it was ten seconds after seeing her in another room, I never knew who I was going to be dealing with—Madame Wonderful or Lady Darth Vader.

Sometimes, though, she could shift into periods of what I call her "best behavior," as I referred to it earlier. For a few days or even up to a few weeks, she'd drink less, be clearer, and be more like a regular mom. Who is this woman, I'd wonder. Why can't she stick around more often? Ohhhh well, I'd think as Lady Darth Vader made her comeback, it was nice while it lasted.

Mom. I loved her. I hated her. Oftentimes that could happen in the same moment.

Dad? Oh, he kept to his woodshop in the garage.

"I think you're expecting way too much from him," my mom said when I'd complain about him. Funny, that's what Dad said about Mom, too, on those rare occasions when I'd open up to him about her.

My older brother kept to his after-school sports and his teams on TV—in every season. I kept to my books and movies. We rarely had friends over to the house.

My mom wasn't a sloppy, over-the-top drinker. In fact, as I mentioned, she was somewhat refined—especially for the blue-collar town I grew up in. But when Cyndi came into my life, drinking a fair bit, it didn't feel that odd to me. In fact, Cyn became even more fun after a few drinks; she didn't have that head-swiveling, neck-breaking personality switch that my mom had. "Whoa—who is she now?" I'd wonder about Mom. Cyndi was just more of her fun, mellow, oozy self.

So here's take two on that earlier thought: okay, well, yes, more than the tea-and-crumpets comment, maybe if I'd paid attention to how much she was drinking, she'd still be alive. But seeing how well it worked to try to make my mom change, I know that would've been useless. Oh, maybe an intervention would've worked, but I didn't think about it. Maybe I was just too habituated to the idea of alcohol being a staple in life that I didn't find it that strange. After all, it wasn't like Cyn was stumbling around frequently. Well, not much, anyway.

Alcohol seemed so mild, genteel almost, compared to what else is so plentiful in this town—drugs, drugs, and more drugs. You name it, someone not too far away can give it. So when Cyndi would be chilling with a chilled glass of wine, it seemed like the least of all the evils, almost lucky. *Ish.*

Actually, I knew there were sleeping and other pills in her medicine cabinet. I tried bringing them up from time to time but talking about them was verboten. I didn't think she took many, but I was probably wrong.

Later that tea-and-crumpets night, she came home with another one. This time it was a woman. I never kept count, but if I had to estimate, in the years that I knew her, she probably came home with hundreds of people. I put blinders on around that, too.

I had a few, too, though. Okay, more than a few but nowhere near a few hundred. Some women here and there, too, and even some mix-and-match stuff (hey, don't give me that—this is LA… and don't tell me you've never wondered; at least I don't have to wonder anymore), but that really wasn't my thing. Women are soft; men are hard. I'm soft; I want hard. I even understand the whole poly and pan thing, but as old-fashioned as it might sound, I like men, one at a time.

The next morning, after the guest had left, I said to Cyn, "I just hope you don't end up dead. Remember *Looking for Mr. Goodbar?*"

Maybe her hangover was a truth serum that morning. "Death has never scared me," she responded. "Living scares me more."

That should've set off more alarm bells than the drinking or the myriad overnight guests. But it didn't.

Shortly after the memorial, her mom told me, "Just stay in the house as long as you want. We'll sell it when you're ready to go."

I loved that house so much—I couldn't imagine ever leaving. I knew it'd have to happen someday, but it wasn't that day yet.

Cyn killed herself in her car with sleeping pills and booze. Maybe she thought the highway-patrol folks were more used to finding such things than maids in hotels rooms or......me. That was very considerate of her toward me, not so much for the highway-patrol folks, as used to this kind of thing as they might be. She also probably wanted to necessitate the least amount of cleanup possible. She was always thoughtful, somewhat, that way.

Thank God she didn't kill herself in the house. I probably couldn't have taken it nor could I have stayed if she'd ended her life there. For the longest time it felt like she was just in the next room. Expecting her to walk in at any moment started to wear on me and probably didn't support me in my grieving much, but I still loved that house. I couldn't handle grieving for two losses at the same time, so I stayed.

It only had two bedrooms, but each bedroom was a master suite with a master bath. If you picked up our (I still call it our) living room and dropped it anywhere else in the country, it might've fit in—if the homeowners were scrumfy, persimmon-y kinds of people. But the thing in our house that was total Hollywood was our bathrooms. They wouldn't fit anywhere else at all except maybe Branson, Missouri. But we loved them. Giant globe lights surrounded the enormous mirrors. Huge, pink powder-puffy rugs tickled our feet. My bathroom always smelled like magic from the oils I put in my bath, in the oversized, clawfoot tub. I felt like a celebrity every time I walked in there.

And, there were flowers. Always. Ever have someone say one thing that affected your life forever? My high-school French teacher did that. *J'aime les fleurs dans la salle de bain.* "I love flowers in the bathroom." Sounds better in French. Everything sounds better in French.

Once I left Wisconsin, forevermore I had flowers in my bathroom. It wasn't just that she said it; it's that flowers in the bathroom are the ultimate. No matter how broke I was, I'd have flowers in my bathroom. It made me feel luxurious. Confucius is quoted as saying that if you have two cents, spend one on food and the other on flowers.

You're right. He probably didn't say that.

Beauty and Brains to Go, Please

By the way, I mentioned earlier that I'm smart, but I didn't tell you how smart. I'm smart...really smart... Mensa qualified. Shhhhhhhh. I know, I know—I should let that show, let it shine, be an example of brains and beauty. But *you* try being smart and beautiful. People HATE you. At least if I acted ditzy, people would assume I was just beautiful and think, "Poor thing. All beauty, no brains." And they'd leave me alone. A little.

One of the problems about being so drop-dead stupid crazy gorgeous (albeit just with makeup; I'm definitely not gorgeous without it), is some people do expect pearls of wisdom to drop from my lips every minute. Sometimes I'd live up to their expectations....but only as a result of the years of being horrendously ugly, when I had to learn to be funny, charming, sharp, and superiorly intellectual. And when I did let pearls of wisdom drop from my lips, I could see different thoughts cross people's faces—as if they'd be thinking, "How is that even fair? No one should get handed that much." And....they'd hate me.

I know, I shouldn't care what people think. But actors are pretty tender creatures. It takes a tender creature to be able to pull from a vat of deep emotions at a moment's notice. It also takes a lot of guts and stamina to try to make it in this town. I figured I'd come out as a smart woman when I'd "made it." Geena Davis is a Mensa member. Meryl Streep is no slouch. Goldie might not act like a smart powerhouse, but she definitely is one.

So people either expect pearls of wisdom to come flowing out of my mouth or they expect absolutely nothing at all. There's very little in between until people get to know me. Mostly the only people, men and women, who would hit on me were those who thought they had nothing to lose. The handsome guys didn't think they had a chance—or thought surely I must have a boyfriend...who could probably beat them to a pulp.

When that techno-geek-chic look came in, I embraced it wholeheartedly. With black-rimmed glasses, people would take me more seriously.

I went to college in Wisconsin for a year, but, as you know, I came to LA when I was nineteen. I finished my degree at UCLA slowly over the years. Looking back, maybe I should've tried Yale Drama—or at least Yale—or something else and done college another way, but I just wanted LA at the time.

I didn't go back to Wisconsin as Cara had suggested, but I did go to Cabo (that's Cabo San Lucas for those who aren't on a first-name basis with it, as if there's only one Cape). That didn't work, because the dozen or so times I'd gone there over the years were with Cyn. Dumb idea.

I went back to LA a few days early and just wandered through my days in a daze and through my daze in the days. I finally went back to work for Skye (the older hippie writer chick who smelled of patchouli) here and there, which was somewhat grounding and gave me a sense of purpose.

Cara slowly started sending me on auditions again, but she stopped when it became obvious I wasn't giving them my all. My all was.....crushed. Plus, I didn't have my cheerleader calling out, "Break a leg!" as I'd leave for an audition. I missed her so much as I'd close the door to the quiet house as I was leaving for yet another cattle call. (I rarely call them that, but they felt like cattle calls at the time...more from my mental state than the actual number of actors they'd call in.) BTW, "break a leg" means "good luck" for actors. It might've come from the idea that actors are so superstitious that they'd think saying "good luck" would yield just the opposite. You know those crazy actors! (Moi?) Another thought is that the curtains on the sides of yesteryear stages were called legs, and to "break a leg" meant a music-hall act was going to be seen, hence paid. I like the first idea better.

Cyn's mom—Janice is her name, just so I can stop calling her Cyn's mom—came to the house so we could go through her stuff and start giving it away. OMG, standing in her room, looking in her closet...it was still like she was in the next room, about to bounce in with a tale of her latest escapade.

We stood there, kind of lost, as we stared at all her gorgeous garments. With her model's body, she could rock just about anything she wore. Radiant, resplendent, ravishing, and, yes, because it deserves to be mentioned twice, rocking—that was Cyn.

"Is there anything you want?"

I reached for her beautiful silk robe and a couple of scarves. Truth be told, I never could wear them.

"I can't do it yet, Trish," Janice said.

"Me either," I responded.

We shut the door to her closet and then to her room.

"Are you sure you're okay with me staying here?" I asked for the umpteenth time. "I can find another place."

"It's fine, honey. Do whatever you need to do." She rushed away. I didn't blame her.

Janice had been hospitalized a few times. "Nerves," was the diagnosis, Cyn had said.

"Nerves?"

"That's what we were told. As if that should've been a good enough answer." Cyn sipped her wine cooler.

Janice finally hired someone to do the clearing-out task for us. It felt like cheating, somehow, but doing the task felt worse. Some random, anonymous woman who didn't know Cyndi at all came and divided her items into throw-away (underwear), give-away (about half of the clothing items), and consignment (the other half). Janice had instructed the woman to give Cyn's red-carpet gowns to a special charity that sells movie-star items. The bedding went into the donation pile, and the anonymous woman put a new comforter on the bed.

I helped her carry everything to her van, trying to get this evil woman out of the house and out of my life as quickly as possible. No, of course she wasn't evil; she was just stealing the last tangible items of Cyn, other than the house itself.

Once the woman flew off on her broom, I sat down on Cyn's bed. "Oh, Cyn," I whispered. "You're still here, aren't you?" The curtain fluttered...but the window was shut and no breeze had come through the house. Great, now I'm seeing things, I thought.

Her three cats rubbed and wrapped themselves around my shins. It was completely unlike her to just leave them—they were her babies. They followed me into the living room and climbed into the chair I was about to sit in. I went to the other chair and they quickly jumped into it. I pretended to start to walk back to the first chair, but quickly sat down as soon as they vacated the second chair. They jumped all over me as soon as they discovered my ruse.

I was glad for their company. I was so lonely, but so not in the mood to talk to anyone. Cats are perfect in that situation.

I've heard it said that when someone loses a spouse, s/he loses not only the spouse part, but also the best friend, confidante, grocery-store pal, driving partner—so many people rolled into one. Cyn wasn't my mate, but she was everything else to me. How did it get to be this way?

Several times an hour I'd reach for my phone to text her about how lousy I was feeling. Remembering I couldn't text her and that she was the reason for my wanting to text her just filled me with tears all over again.

I wandered all the way through Whole Foods and realized I hadn't put anything in my cart. There—peanut butter. I added some crackers, too, since some of the feedback Cara was getting from the casting directors was that I looked too drawn and haggard. They were organic, non-GMO peanut butter and crackers, of course.

I sat in the little café section of the store with my so-called lunch and people watched. I tell you, the characters in this town are not just in the movies. They're everywhere. I suppose that's anywhere, really. The characters in my small hometown are just as loopy as the ones in LA, myself included. Both places. All places. We're a strange bunch, we humans—anywhere you tend to find us.

There was the store manager I worked for who had her sweatshirts dry-cleaned, and her nails were perfectly manicured. But she was enormous. There was so much dedication to one area of her life and so much lack of dedication in another. I know, I know—obesity is like a disease, like alcoholism, like diabetes. We certainly wouldn't judge someone for having diabetes (well, some would, but anyway) so we can't judge people for their weight. But I just found her fascinating.

On top of being crazy characters themselves, people in my acting classes also smelled quite interesting. The baristas smelled like coffee. The caterers smelled like chicken cordon bleu. One guy smelled like socks—worn socks, that is. I never wanted to get close enough to him to ask about his life to determine why he smelled like socks. Hopefully I didn't smell too much like a Zumba-class teacher or whatever I was up to at that moment. If I smelled like hanging out at Skye's house, which would make me smell like patchouli, too, that'd be fine, I guess.

Even more crazy were the characters I dated. I've met tons of fellas at the Screen Actors Guild movie screenings, but actors really aren't my favorite guys to date. Some weird competition thing would start to happen when one or the other of us would get more auditions and/or roles.

There was the roadie whose tailpipe dragged on the road behind his dilapidated car. But he made his bed with perfect hospital corners. I'm all for hospital corners, but it just seemed totally incongruous. What makes us decide which idiosyncrasy to hang our hat on?

Then there was Johnson who didn't seem to have enough sense to turn his name into a genuine first name, let alone something that didn't imply *dick*—which he was. Oh, I try to be kind and give people the benefit of the doubt, but after doing that time and again with him, I finally surmised that he reveled in his dickness, his dickocity. He would have used the word surmise, not realizing that using erudite (there I go again, using a word he would've used) words outside of an academic setting doesn't make people sound smart; it makes them sound pretentious and insecure, because insecurity is what makes people pretentious.

He was amazingly handsome; too bad he was so aware of it. One time he actually said, "I am so friggin' vain. As well I should be!"

Then there was the super-rich guy....and the other one....and the other...and even that one with the Richard Branson hairdo, although he wasn't that old. At least it wasn't the Trump hair-...whatever that is. It's certainly not a hair*do*—more like a hairdither. Orange is the new...blue (hair, blood...okay maybe it's not that funny). Back to my rich guys: they were so into how it all looked, not how it all was. The emphasis was on that oh-so-(not-so-very)-serious swag. And part of how it all looked was to have a beautiful date. Cyndi definitely had the same problem. Talk about mansplaining though—they had advanced degrees in that. Ugh! They liked to consider themselves masters of the universe, but they might've been the only ones who did. They could've been such great guys if they could've just calmed the frig down, if they hadn't been pretending so much.

Hey, I heard that. Yes, actors pretend, too. But we have to dig deep to draw on real emotions in order for audiences to believe us. I'm going to humblebrag for all of us here. My spellcheck didn't even question that word, so I guess it's really an established thing now. Hollywood is known as a fake, make-believe world, but bah! If we're not feeling those feelings, you won't either, and you're who we're doing this for...at least somewhat, after ourselves first, because it's what we love and live to do.

Back to my love (not so much) life. Then there was the Uber driver...and the other Uber driver...and the other Uber driver...and the other....although not necessarily in that order, LOL. Actually, they were intermingled with the rich guys. Then there was the guy I had to get a restraining order for. And the other. Fortunately the order worked with both of them, and they disappeared before they became full-on stalker nightmares. Plus there was the Burning Man guy and the dreadlocks guy and the man-bun guy. He was some Silver Lake hipster back when that was the thing. He was a little younger, which was especially nice after all those older rich guys, but I'm not into long beards and man buns. It takes a really special guy to carry off that look successfully, and he wasn't and didn't.

There was Mr. It-Is-What-It-Is Guy. I mean it is what it is, all right, but I didn't have to be reminded every five minutes.

It might sound like a lot, and I did date a fair bit, but I really only averaged one relationship a year for a few months over the twenty-odd years I've been in LA. They never lasted very long. Now I know why, but I didn't at the time.

Oh, people. What a wild bunch we are. Quiet and scared of our shadows. Outrageously flamboyant to hide that we're scared of our shadows. Worried, obsessive, OCD, tightly wound—that was me. Drippy and oozy and gorgeous and melodramatic crossed with easygoing, yet suicidal—that was Cyn.

I quickly put on my sunglasses to cover my tears. Cyn, Cyn, Cyn.

CHAPTER 4

Fifty Shades of Orange

October is always orange. No matter where I am in the world—at least in the Northern Hemisphere—October comes in orange. Wisconsin is a pumpkin orange. Bordeaux, France, is a soft orange. Northern California is a gentle orange. Florida is a bold orange. Russia, China, Japan—they're all their own oranges.

How did I get lucky enough to travel to so many places? Well, without much makeup and with brown or blonde hair color, I can look a whole range of oddball characters, from a crack addict to a hillbilly to a psych-ward patient to a prostitute. So I actually get a lot of work as unknown, unmemorable characters. I'm the loud, ugly, angry woman in the crowd behind a lynching (ugh!) or a burning at the stake (ugh!). It's a good thing I can look so unmemorable because I can keep getting roles like this.

With my hair in a ponytail, I can be a soccer mom, the best friend, or an infomercial fitness maven. Hair in a bun and I'm suddenly the understanding teacher or the loving aunt; add old-fashioned glasses and I become the meek secretary who knows her boss's dark secrets. With more makeup and a sophisticated hairdo, I transform into the rich socialite or the smarmy couture director. Add glasses and I can become a kind professor, a museum curator, a bank executive. Actually, the older I get, the more roles I can do.

Truthfully, though, sometimes the makeup thing makes me feel, well, made up—the false kind...the being-a-fraud kind. Without it I go invisible because my eyelashes disappear, and most of what makes me striking is involved in my eyes, which only really show up with mascara, eyeliner, and eyeshadow. People have actually gasped when they've seen me without makeup when they're used to seeing my full Hollywood face. Even my laptop doesn't recognize me without makeup! Oh, well. Here I am—the lashless wonder until the magic wand of mascara has had its way with my long (but light red) eyelashes. I heard it said once (and I'm not sure it was straight from the source) that Cindy Crawford doesn't even look like Cindy Crawford when she wakes up in the morning. Few supermodels look fabulous without their face put on. That made me feel better, a little less fraudulent. But still....

Back to the orange hue of October, LA has the best orange of all. I love LA, especially in October, but I love leaving it, too, so I can come back and love it again. As you know by now, the constant striving wears me down after a while.

One of the oddest things about me is that it's easier for me to go to India than it is to go to the post office. It's easier for me to go scuba diving than to buy a packet of stamps. Regarding going to India, I'm talking everything—go get a passport picture taken for the visa, stand in line for hours at the consulate, buy the plane ticket, fly eighteen hours in a cramped airplane seat to the other side of the world, stand in line again. And that's just the beginning—everything requires standing in line there. I'm also talking getting Delhi Belly and talking to and feeding lepers in the street.

Scuba diving requires getting to the place, putting on your gear....well, you get the idea. Meanwhile, the post office is just down the street. It even has a parking lot. I can't explain myself.

One time I was sitting in an auto rickshaw in India watching an older woman line up her few possessions on the sidewalk, sweep out her little makeshift tent with a tiny broom, and start putting the items back. She could sense someone was watching her, and she looked over at me with (what I took to be) fierce indignation and pride.

I wish I could have told her that I was admiring how much reverence she treated each object with. Moments like that put everything in perspective, for a while, until it wears off. And then I'm back to the LA striving thing along with everyone else.

But one thing is for sure—my travels make me love my adopted town all the more. As I ride the airport bus, there are those palm trees, lifting my heart anew. The palm trees in Viet Nam and Thailand and Australia and Florida lift my heart, too, but somehow this is different.

As I lay in bed looking out at the beautiful orange hue of LA in October, however, I wondered if I'd ever have energy to get up and go to China (for example, and no small feat) again. I pulled myself together to head over to Skye's once a week. That was something, at least.

OMG, did I miss the Emmys? When were they? What happened to September? Was I even alive last month? What about last summer? What in the world did I do? I don't even remember the Fourth of July. Cyn and I used to go to a restaurant up in the higher hills of Glendale and watch bunches of fireworks displays off in the distance...all while huddling around a fire pit, snuggled up with people we didn't even know because the wind up there was bone chilling.

Most of my friends stopped calling. I guess they were tired of suggesting things to do only to have me say no over and over. I would do a like-storm on Facebook— liking everything in sight...something would really have to suck for me to not like it—just to let them know I was still around and cared for them. I just didn't want to see them.

I have a few thousand friends on Facebook. Okay, maybe a few hundred are people I'm pretty close to— friends, family, special coworkers. But I do care about all few thousand of them.

My high-school class has a FB page, and every now and then someone posts about a classmate who'd died. I'd look at the pictures of who the person evolved to over the course of his or her life and what people wrote about him or her. I looked them up again, knowing each one of them probably had someone like me crying her eyes out about him or her.

As I scrolled through Facebook, all those stupid, friggin' memes that say things like "A broken heart is how the light gets in" made me want to scream, "Fuck you!" My attitude needed some help, that was for sure. The ones that said things like "Don't quit your daydream" or "Goal Digger" made me smile…a little bit.

Even my nighttime dreams had changed. That recurring bad dream that so many actors have—that it's opening night and we realize we hadn't memorized our lines well enough—had faded. Non-acting friends have recurring bad dreams, too, perhaps about showing up for a final and realizing they hadn't studied well enough. My dreams of late seemed to involve whispers and angels and Cyn, somehow. I didn't remember them well enough…as soon as I'd realize I was awake, even if Cyn wasn't clearly in my mind, my heart would say, "Something's wrong. What is it? Where's the pain coming from?" And thoughts of Cyn would flood in. The dreams popped like soda bubbles.

Cara called about an audition for a role I could actually do—a mom whose child dies. Plus it had twelve lines in a movie being filmed in the Philippines, and it was filming right away. The woman who was supposed to be the mom got very sick, and the casting director was in a state.

"The CD wants you off book," Cara said. "Can you do that?" Translated, that means the casting director wanted me to have my lines memorized.

Well, usually I can be off book just fine. "Sure," I said, although this time does not fall under the doing anything "just fine" category. Cara sent me the "sides" (the part of the script I'd be reading from) and I tried to start memorizing them. Emphasis on tried.

Dressing for auditions is the easiest thing to dress for. If it's for a teacher, I dress like a teacher—slacks, blouse, soft and slouchy cardigan. If it's for a detective, I dress like that—slacks, jacket, blouse, black glasses. An overwrought, stay-at-home mom? Sweatshirt and leggings, hair in a sloppy ponytail. A best friend? Jeans and a fun, not-too-colorful-so-I don't-outshine-the-star top.

Other than auditions and parties, including opening nights, I live in my workout gear, although it's usually the trendiest I can find since I still have an image to keep up...if only to myself, LOL. My jackets and shirts cover my butt, though, which is too skinny to be fashionable. But if I plump it up, the rest of me gets too plump. Sometimes I can find leggings with booty padding, but that feels dumb. My mom and aunts aren't very skinny, but they have the skinny white-girl's butt that I inherited.

I dragged myself to the studio and got the part. They didn't even care that I wasn't completely off book—this was the first and only audition where I didn't have the lines memorized. I guess in my bedraggled state I really looked the part of a mom whose child dies.

Then I dragged myself to the Philippines, which had a tinge of orange. Then I dragged myself home, which included a moment on the plane.

I'd fallen asleep, kind of. In that in-between-awake-and-asleep state, I was thinking of going home to my beautiful city with the perfect weather, to my beautiful home, to my wonderful friend and roommate.

"Oh, no!" I'm not sure I said it out loud. The people around me were dozing, so it must've just been in my head. Some enormous wave of something or other shot up from my gut, and I was wide awake and ready to start screaming or wailing or both.

Pleaseohpleaseohpleasedon'tletmescreamonthisplane pleasedon'tletmescreamonthisplanepleasedon'tletmescr eamonthisplanepleasedon'tletmescreamonthisplane.

All those years of breathing lessons in my acting classes kicked in, and I just slowly breathed through my nose and deep into my belly and slowly out through my mouth.

Back home, I fell back into bed. But at least I did something; it was a start—or restart as the case might've been.

This Thing I Lugged Around

I remember a friend mentioning that, after she lost her husband, folks told her to make sure she got dressed every day. That helps stave off depression—or, perhaps more accurate, not getting dressed adds to depression. Around my house the getting-dressed thing wasn't saying very much. Cyn and I would often wander around in lingerie. We didn't wear anything totally see-through and robes were always at the ready in case one of us got a package, but it made us feel very sexy and Hollywood. It saved on AC, too.

I hadn't done the lingerie thing since Cyn died. But once my jetlag wore off (it's always worse going East), I put on my favorite crimson lacey thing.

A few days later, I hauled that skinny butt of mine to the gym. I'd stopped going. Thankfully the grieving-mother role didn't require much in the way of buffness. What it did require—wanness, pallor, and a broken heart—I had plenty of. I still finally dragged myself to the gym because my body had started to ache more than my heart. Wow— that's a lot of ache.

Speaking of bahhh-dy, my fingers drummed to the Justin Timberlake song as I drove to the gym. BTW, if you're wondering why I don't actually quote song lyrics, authors really can't do that these days without a whole lot of legal hooha.

I was actually feeling good for a little bit. Then my brain, not always my most helpful ally, reminded me that my best friend died and was gone forever, I'd never see her again, and it was all my fault because I should have seen it coming and done something from my Wonder Woman arsenal to ward it off. Nothing could make me cray cray like my own mind. My heart went back to its new regular resting place, grief.

But, hey! Cyndi wasn't the first thing I thought of when I woke up that morning, for the first time in seven months. That's not entirely accurate….as I mentioned a bit ago, sometimes even if I didn't think of her by name immediately, my slowly waking-up-for-the-day mind knew there was some big hurt lurking on the sidelines, waiting to rush in. What was it? Oh….right.

But the rushing-in of the hurt didn't happen that morning, at least not right away. That's something.

How in the world did seven months just go by? Where was I? What was I? Not awake much, that's for sure. How could I have not worked out for seven months? That's the most unlike me thing ever in the history of ever. Seven months seems like an eternity, and it also seems like I just woke up from a long winter's nap or something.

"Whaaaaaaat?" my arms yelled as I lifted a few weights far below what I'd been lifting last spring. "Heeeeyyyyyy!" my legs groaned as I attempted high-intensity interval training on the cardio machines. Beastmode I was not.

Over the years my workouts have grown shorter as my food intake has grown larger. Nowadays the guideline has shifted to eat more, exercise less—well, the right kind of eating and the right kind of exercising: that is, not starving and not spending hours on cardio. I follow a high-fat/low-carb diet (Keto, not Paleo); for exercise I focus on weight lifting and high-intensity interval training (HIIT). Works for me.

After my workout, I caught a glimpse of myself in the mirror on the wall. Forget that—the walls are mirrors in this place...I guess they figure we need all the encouragement we can get, including seeing our out-of-shape bods full out. But...was that a sparkle? I hadn't seen one of those in a while. A couple of fellows smiled at me as I left. Am I back, I wondered. Maybe it was just that I was finally looking up instead of down.

One time I saw someone rant in the comments under a Facebook weight-loss ad, "Don't you know that we don't all care about looking like celebrities?" No. I didn't know that. Growing up watching every movie ever made (or trying to), I wanted nothing else than to look like a movie star. It's so strange how my wish came so true. Maybe if I'd put *be* a movie star into the thought mix, things would've worked out better for me....but that was really beyond my wildest dreams for most of my childhood. And...there's still time.

But, no. When an entire career can hinge on one blemish or five extra pounds, and said career is what I've been living for, no, that thought never occurred to me.

Before LA, I actually had no idea how to move around in this thing—this body thing, I mean. Every morning when I wake up, I feel like I've been gajillions of light-years away, and I have to come back and move around in this thing that's so crazy clunky. I actually had to take body lessons, such as Feldenkrais and the Alexander Technique. You name it, I probably tried it.

I come alive and I'm so graceful when I'm swimming or dancing. But just walking or that standing-up-straight thing? Ix-nay! I wasn't so good at those regular human (for other people) activities. I had to take lessons on how to put one foot in front of the other...gracefully, not like a mother rhino charging to protect her baby. And, oh! To stand up straight—what's that? Before all this work, I was the missing link: hunched over, almost like a human question mark. In my snippier moods when I'd catch the reflection in a window or mirror of my curled-over body, I'd wonder, "Why don't you just go all the way and bend over and walk with your hands on the ground?" I had to unfold my body, which wasn't easy.

I had some help, though. One day I had a neck and shoulder spasm that was so bad I considered going to the ER. I went to my chiropractor instead, and she promptly fixed whatever had gotten out of whack. The pain would return when I started to hunch and slunch, so my career as the missing link was effectively over.

Another thing that really helped was hearing a personal trainer say, "Put your deltoids in your back pocket." I'd heard lines like "lift your heart" and "tits to God," which are really great and worked for a while, but for some reason the deltoids comment stuck. I think I'd been trying to put my delts in my front pocket before.

Actually, it was easier when I was pudgy and less than attractive. No one had any expectations, least of all me. But, still...maybe it was because I was so desperately unattractive, homely—okay, let's say it again, fugly—as a child, that finally looking like a celebrity was badass. Being celebrated for how I look was a whole lot better than overhearing my aunt tell my mom, "Wait a few more years. She'll grow into herself." That sure hurt, but hearing her say, "See? I told you so!" to my mom a few years later was a bit of a salve.

At first my body became a twenty-four-hour obsession, a never-ending job. It never becomes all perfect, of course, but I liked being as close to my version of perfect as possible. My weight is an intricate balance. If I get too skinny, I look gaunt and no one wants that, unless a part specifically calls for it. But if I weigh too much, I look a little bloated or puffy on screen.

Water helps. I drink so much friggin' water that I intimately know every single bathroom in town, especially between my house and Cara's office.

But once I got my body used to being in shape, it became a project, a spiritual practice instead of an obsession. Some people have daily devotions and meditations.

I had daily workouts—well, daily for six days a week. On the seventh day I rested, had a massage (no matter *how* broke I was, as I've said), sat in a sauna or a whirlpool, or took a long bath with a mixture of organic olive oil and essential oils, specifically Bulgarian Rose Oil, bought after the odd high-paying gig.

One thing I quickly found out about being quite thin was that having such a low body-fat count meant that I was cold. Constantly. As in *all* the time. I bought a down jacket in a little pouch that I carried in a tote bag for when I was sitting in artic restaurants or casting rooms or waiting on set for the scene. The crew gets so hot working around all those lights that they have to blast the AC in there to the point where they could probably breed penguins and polar bears. The longer I was in LA, the more I wore that jacket. Here I was from Wisconsin where I used to wear a T-shirt when it was thirty out, and suddenly I was like one of those Malibu babes wearing a down vest and ugg boots when it was sixty out. But, I tell you, those ocean breezes can feel colder than a Wisconsin snowfall sometimes. It sinks into the bones more somehow.

Fat was once an enemy, something to fight off, but it's actually become easier and easier to keep it at bay. My ankles and knees hurt when I'm carrying even just five extra pounds. Personally, I think obesity is from the GMOs—that and the pesticides that are mashed into everything. They (whoever *they* are again) want to shove fake food down people's throats, literally. The masses are easier to control when they're fat, sick, addicted, and staring at a TV or computer screen. GMOs didn't start out as a bad thing—people wanted a heartier grain to feed the whole world. That's certainly not bad.

But the usual farmer, according to my mother, a Midwest farmer's daughter, doesn't do the GMO or the pesticide thing. They can't afford it. The small farmers save the best part of their crop to plant again in the fall for next year's crop. They don't buy seeds from the big

GMO goons. And pesticides? Most of the smaller farmers can't afford it.

I'm also a foodie, even a gourmet cook, if you will. If I had to evacuate my house because of a fire (not a far-fetched thing to plan for in this part of the world), I'd grab my wok and knives before any jewelry. Actually, I *was* a foodie and gourmet cook and I am again now. I'll explain the hiatus later on.

Cyndi ate junk. Then she exercised her derrière off. Most cows are fed garbage, literally; so she was—as many, many others were and are—eating garbage, literally. How can anyone expect to feel good when s/he's just eaten a hamburger made from a cow that was fed trash?

One time I was reaching for some milk in the dairy section of the grocery store, and something or someone literally spoke in my brain: "You know cows are given bovine growth hormone, don't you?" My hand stopped in midair. And that growth hormone isn't exactly strained out of their milk, I thought, so it'd have to go into me. If it makes the cow bigger, it'd do the same thing to me, wouldn't it? I reached for the organic milk from grass-fed cows, plus I stopped shopping at regular grocery stores. It hurt my heart to see folks filling their carts with fake food and sweets and such on their way to refill their high-blood-pressure meds.

"Waddya think that's doing to you?" I once asked Cyn as she put her artificial creamer and sweetener in her coffee and bit into an egg sandwich from a place that smells like French fries.

Cyn, if only you could come back, I'd buy you a burger. And fries. And even a shake. Okay, maybe not. But I should've made an extra green goop, as you called it, for you every morning while I made my smoothie.

I've been a compassionate eater for years. I wish I could be a vegetarian—hell, I feel bad when I accidentally kill a bug. But when I'd try to go veg, then I couldn't think straight or even get out of bed after two days. So I eat as little meat as possible and make sure every serving of meat is a compassionate one (eggs from free-range chickens, beef from cows that receive their daily massage.... okay, maybe not that extreme, but you get the idea). I finally convinced her to eat a few compassionate meals a week, but she probably did it to shut me up, be companionable, and enjoy a meal where she didn't have to sit in the drive-through by herself more than for any other reason. (Our meal was still take-out, but not from a fast-food place.)

One thing Cyndi would let me help her with was workouts. I'd get her free passes to whatever class I was teaching. Meanwhile, she helped me with makeup and hair shades and dressing. We'd bop through the shops on Melrose, and she'd take completely unrelated items— scarves, clunky jewelry, a floofy top, crazy shoes—and turn them into a fashion statement.

She always leaned toward form-fitting with low necklines. Ack. When I first hung out with her, I leaned toward XXL T-shirts and sweatshirts. I mentioned that my figure figured itself out and I took excellent care of it, but that didn't mean I always strutted it proudly.

"Show us what you got there, girl!" Cyn admonished me at least a thousand times. "What else did you come to this town for if not to show the world who you are and what you have?"

As for a pair of tatas in the bodacious category (Quick, what movie is that line—or close to it—in? Yes, you got it: *An Officer and a Gentleman*), Cyn had 'em. She should've, as she paid enough for them.

One time we both were on diets. I don't usually diet (I've had so many friends mess up their metabolism—and lives—with diets and diet drugs), but I had to fit into a certain costume. And because I don't usually diet, they really work when I do. Ugh—but what happens on a diet? All I thought about was food! That makes sense—deprive the body of something and suddenly that's all it wants.

We were lounging in the living room watching TV and trying not to think about food. But what does TV love to advertise? Food, food, and more food. Then it advertises weight-loss products as well as pharmaceuticals that wouldn't be necessary if society wasn't getting drunk on junk food. Great racket they have going on there. Actually, it's amazing society does as well as it does, given the rot our minds and bodies are served.

After the third ad for pizza and potato chips and whatever, we both leapt off the sofa and ran to the fridge. I was stark raving hungry, but whether it was from the diet or all those ads while I was on the diet, I wasn't sure.

"Is there any chocolate anywhere?" I screamed.

"Yes, yes, here." Cyndi pulled some chocolate cookies out of the freezer and popped them in the microwave to melt a bit. I don't typically do microwaves, but this was a special exception.

"Beam me up, Scotty," I said after we ate alllllll of those cookies and my stomach was more than a little confused.

"There might not be any chocolate up there."

"Okay, never mind—I'll stay here. But remind me to never eat like this again."

Cyn probably made herself throw up after that. She did that from time to time. I hate throwing up, so that wasn't my thing. But I can't say I never did it—especially after some party where the host would've been insulted if we didn't eat the gluten- and sugar-laden fare. The problem with hearing about Princess Diana and others being bulimic is that it made it more approachable: "Well, if she does it, and she's who she is, someone like lowly old me could certainly do it."

I was usually pushed to eat more by one of those rich boyfriends at a swanky gala. Nowadays I would just say, "No, thanks." It took me a long time to come into my "No." It took even longer to come into my full "Yes."

Since my usual food plan is somewhat limited in the treats department, the one special luxury I've allowed myself is coffee. I get high on it, I get off on it, I go crazy over it. During my less-than-no-money phases I'd live on coffee and chewing gum. A character Carol Burnett played in a movie mentioned that, and I thought it sounded like a great idea for taming the hunger pangs. It really works.

Now I only drink fair trade and organic (at home, anyway; at airports and on the road, it's catch as catch can). Coffee is apparently pretty good for us. And if you tell me about a study that says coffee is bad for us, I'm going to stick my fingers in my ears and go lalalalalalalalalaaaaaa and then nanananananananaaaaa.

Cyndi and I would frequent coffee shops—that was one of our favorite things to do together. This year, though, I couldn't go into one until Thanksgiving time. The call of the pumpkin-spice latte, which would be out of season soon, was greater than the dread of going into a coffee shop...without her. Before she died, I'd go to them by myself all the time. After, it was a heartache. I grabbed my pumpkin-spice latte and ran out the door.

Finding Center

Another start was going back to my spiritual center. I found an amazing, dynamic spiritual community years earlier, although God wasn't really my thing. Life—that's Life with a capital L, even when it's not at the start of a sentence—is. I remember hearing the minister say once, "A rose blooming on a hillside lifts up the whole world. And that's its job, its purpose, its impact." When the acting thing (or lack thereof) got me down, I'd remember those words, and just ponder the idea that my main job in life is to be a rose. To me that means to live full out and be kind, genuine, a good friend—basically be as loving as I can as often as I can.

I took on a special project there: I'd send spiritual books and magazines to prisoners all over the country. I'd get into a zone of such love and peace as I wrote the letters and put together the packages for people I didn't know, both men and women. The packages grew into the hundreds over the few years. The folks often wrote back, sometimes with questions, which I'd answer as best I could, and a correspondence grew.

Actors are actually very spiritual people. In our circles we had a lot of Buddhists plus a lot of New Thought/Ancient Wisdom folks. Various boyfriends would take me to the Self-Realization Fellowship. Others would take me to their form of church—hiking in the hills. Sometimes the tree branches stretching overhead really felt cathedralesque. It's all good.

Actors have to be spiritual, really, if you ask me. People accuse us of being shallow, of having to play other roles because we can't play ourselves in the world. But we do play ourselves in the world. And, as I've said, we have to dig deep into a well of emotions, which can be unpleasant if not downright scary at times, to play some roles.

Also, it's hard to be in the public eye. For the very famous, every human foible is blown up. Imagine if that one bad day you were having last month made its way around cyberspace. Just a wayward glance can be turned into an affair. We're always judged by the outside. It takes an unbelievable amount of stamina on the inside to withstand that. So we have to dive deep.

Truthfully, all of us have to dive deep to withstand the insanity on this planet; with almost eight billion of us, we have almost eight billion ways of diving deep. Sometimes it's dumpster diving, though—drugs, alcohol, too much food, addiction to our gadgets being some of the ways we plunge into that dumpster.

Speaking of dumpster diving, although this is more literal, one time I played a homeless person in a friend's movie. Three of us with make-up dirt smeared on our faces sat on a sidewalk in downtown San Francisco. The film crew had to go around the corner to start the scene, so the three of us were just sitting there. An older couple walking down the sidewalk crossed the street to avoid us, and then crossed back after they passed us.

Wow. My heart went out to every homeless person I'd ever rendered less-than or invisible. Even if I don't give them money, which I do from time to time, I still look at them to let them know I see them. They're here. They're important. They matter.

Homeless folks. Prisoners. Actors. We're all Life's children. We're all here for each other.

Cyn had been raised Lutheran, like so many of my neighbors.

"I sure wish we had social time like the Lutherans," I once joked. "The Episcopalians had theirs, too. So did the Pentecostals. Everyone else, really. I wonder why the Catholics didn't."

"But as a Lutheran you would've had to deal with being told things like 'Pride cometh before the fall, Miss Know-It-All.'" Cyn said the quote in a shrill voice, imitating her mother.

"Geez, whenever I act all high and mighty, Life comes along and kind of kicks me down pretty right quick. Didn't that ever happen to her?"

"Oh, sure. But she didn't—still doesn't—know to attribute it to that. She just thinks kick-downs are her own rotten luck."

"One thing I appreciate about Catholicism is being absolved of sin. I mean, it's ridiculous, of course—no other human can do that for anyone else, really. But it's a nice idea, this clean-slate thing."

"I'd love a clean slate," Cyn muttered.

One night she came home and started screaming. I mean…screaming—as in bloody murder. She screamed and screamed and screamed and screamed. When her throat grew hoarse, she started sobbing. And sobbing. And sobbing.

After all the screaming and sobbing subsided, one word came out. "Daddy."

Cyn's dad died when she was three. She had vague memories of this bigger-than-life John Wayne character saving her day.

One time as I was trying to hurry her out of the house, I yelled, "Daylight's burning!" She burst into tears. She'd seen every John Wayne movie at least a dozen times. I never said it to her again. That line is one of my favorites of all time, but I reserved it for other friends.

So the person she called "Dad" for the past thirty years was really her stepfather. She didn't want to call him Dad, but her mother was so insistent on creating that happy-family storybook-picture thing after those years of agonizing grief, that Cyn just went along with it. But she felt like doing that was betraying her memory of the one she wanted to call Dad.

"Cyn, you can love two people without betraying either," I told her, but she didn't hear me.

She came from some serious money, too. "The problem with coming from money is everyone expects you to be happy," she once said, "and when you're not, it's like what the hell is wrong with you? It's even like, how dare you? You know how many people in the world—even in this town—are hungry and would love to trade places with you for even one hour?"

"Hmmmmmmmm," I said because I had no idea what to say.

"People say, 'Oh, must've been nice.' Or, 'Gee, I would've loved to have traded problems.' Or, 'Oh, just give me a chance to see what it was like.'"

"Hmmmmmmmmm," I said again because those three lines definitely had crossed my mind more than a few times as she never struggled to pay her bills and I did from time to time.

Oh, Life. We all have our gremlins and demons in there. We're all living a tragedy at times. What made hers so unbearable? Was it the perfect storm of still not feeling like she'd "made it," being dumped, and turning forty in the toughest town on Earth on top of unresolved childhood stuff and eating garbage and popping pills and drinking and….?

Humans are such strange animals. I fret and babble—at least in my head, if not outwardly all the time; that's one of my main coping mechanisms. Cyn's coping mechanisms included a penchant for the macabre.

I'd gush about the Hollywood sign. "Yeah, strange how Peg Entwistle, a young actress, jumped to her death from the H in 1932" was the merry response from my bestie. I'd gush about living by the ocean someday. "Didn't a quarter million people die in that tsunami back in '04?" was the response to that. I'd laugh at how Californians call the brown hillsides "golden." (They can be green in the late winter and early spring from the rains—yes, it rains here, contrary to popular belief—but that's it.) "Yeah, they're fucking brown," she'd grumble. You get the idea.

"Oh, Cyn," I'd say. "Oh, Cyn," I was still saying. She wasn't always like that, of course…but now she'd always be like this: dead. "Talk about killing it, Cyn," I said out loud. God, I sounded just like her.

Grief is an even stranger animal than humans. I would be driving along, happy as a lark, and suddenly out of nowhere, up from the depths of my being—completely without warning—would come these crazy racking sobs. But that was usually just in the safety and solitude of my car, mostly, or the house sometimes. One time it happened in a store, and that was a little embarrassing. The sales staff understood just one word: "Died." They looked at the phone in my hand (where it lives, usually) and thought I'd just received word of a dear friend or relative's death. I let them think that.

Other cultures have sitting shiva or keening or stuff. The Irish tell jokes and get drunk. At least my Irish family did that when someone died. (Well, no, we didn't do that when Brian died.)

Maybe if I'd cried more in the beginning, I could've avoided these crazy moments. But as quickly as they came, they'd go. What the hell was that?

No, Cyn wasn't a partner, a lover; she wasn't blood family, but we were the sister neither of us ever had—the one we'd been waiting for. Does that make sense? Plus, each new loss brings up the old ones. Even moving can be a loss that brings up the old ones.

Maybe a good metaphor for grief is water, specifically an ocean with high tides and low, ebbs and flows. One day the winds bring white caps; another day it's completely calm. It'd been eight months already, so I'd have a few decent days and think, okay, cool, I'm getting through this. But then a supermoon rose and the high tide rushed in. The waves caught me off guard and knocked me down; I couldn't breathe as I tumbled over and over. I was swept up on to the shore, getting scratched by the sand, panting for air.

Despite the unhappy metaphor, my go-to spot was still the beach. I once heard on a blogtalk show that the cheapest, easiest way to get yourself healthy is to just put your bare feet on the bare ground. "Earthing," the naturopathic doc called it. And of course the farther away from the cell-phone and WiFi vibes, the better—and not on grass freshly sprinkled with weed killer, either.

So there's a formal name for one of my favorite things to do, go to the beach and stick my feet in the sand. All the problems of the world melt away. The sun sinks into the ocean—or a fogbank—and the troubles evaporate.

I started going to Leo Carillo beach to hang out with the dogs, literally. I loved Cyn's cats, but I'm much more of a dog person. This way I could enjoy all that exuberant dog energy without having all that responsibility. Plus, this beach has crags and caves…that'd be me at this particular time of my life—craggy and cavey.

"Hi, Patricia."

I looked up, but because the sunset was behind this unknown man, I couldn't see his face. Not many people would be able to recognize me with sunglasses on and my hair completely tucked up into a baseball hat.

A furry face was suddenly right in mine. No, not his, but one belonging to a shaggy, gorgeous, exceedingly friendly dog. She was so friendly, in fact, it seemed like she wanted to crawl inside my body to share it with me.

He sat down beside me, trying to rein in his dog and keep her from becoming one with my face, but his phone rang. "Oh, sorry! I've got to dash!"

And away he dashed. Who in the world was that? Who knows my real name? Must've been someone from a movie, because I do use Patricia in the credits, so folks on set (logically) think that's what they should call me. But I haven't used it anywhere else since Wisconsin.

CHAPTER 5

A Blue Christmas, I'll Have

I'm going a little Yoda on you in that title because of that legal thang with lyrics. Anyway, about that Christmas thang....

I always always always always loved Christmas. Well, maybe not the year the dog ate the guinea pig—that one not so much. But the others were magical times. I adore it, revel in it, deck the halls, and all that jazz. I love the lights, the trees, the wrapped packages.

That's the one time of the year I remember Dad actually playing the piano, and we'd all sing carols. Mom would nip the eggnog a bit too much, but it was a happy time.

Cyndi hated Christmas. It got so bad that she'd go to some beach in Thailand with her latest guy for the holidays. She couldn't avoid Christmas altogether there, though, because the hotel owners would put up trees, thinking the *farangs* (foreigners) would want a touch of Christmas and home.

"If I wanted a touch of Christmas and home, I would've stayed home!" Cyn would grumble.

I never left LA over the holidays—I got more auditions from the middle of November to the beginning of January than I would in the six months before and after. Most actors go home to lick their wounds and come back refreshed, due in part to the accolades from their friends and family. As I said before, my circle back in Wisconsin would just look at me with that why-haven't-you-made-it-yet look. "I might be a hometown beauty," I'd want to tell them. "But I'm average for Los Angeles." That might not have been taken too well, so I just kept that to one myself.

On Christmas Eve I'd go to a special service at my spiritual center. One time the band played "Breath of Heaven" while an eight-month-pregnant woman danced. I'm not much into the story of the Virgin Birth and all, but that was one enchanted moment as she whirled around celebrating life, love, and new birth. On Christmas Day, my latest huggahunk and I would pick up Cara, and we'd go off to a huge orphan Christmas party comprised of numerous folks who don't have family in LA.

That year was a completely different story. Christmas sucks when you're single *and* your BFF just offed herself. That year I was with Cyndi—with her hatred of Christmas, that is. I actually checked prices for overseas trips, but it was too close to Christmas to get any decent fares. Four thousand dollars to fly to India—wow! Luckily, Cara sent me on more and more auditions as my strength was returning...somewhat.

December and January are the two months of the year in SoCal when the heat might click on, bringing warm memories of home. That and the smell of a dryer running and baked goods coming out of the oven fill me with memories that are all misty and maybe even water-colored....of things that probably weren't the way they were in my mind. Plus, the one baking the Christmas cookies and banana bread was me, not Mom.

Speaking of memories that are all misty and maybe even watercolored, as I told you earlier, I listen to love songs along with all those dedications between family members or couples who just met or were celebrating thirty-odd years. And I cry a little, or sometimes even a lot. Even when I was dating some guy, I knew there was someone special for me, and I wasn't with him yet. But every love song brought me closer to him—whoever he was, wherever he was, doing whatever he was doing.

I'm so happy to hear that he's just a single call away, that maybe once in my life I'll find that someone who really does need me, that Annie replenishes his senses like I could do in the right place, in the right time, and with the right person. (You know the right words to all of those.)

One night near the end of her life, I arrived home singing that song. Cyndi was sitting on the deck, drink in hand.

"I want to know who Annie is and why making love to her was like a night in the woods or a sleepy blue sea or a walk in the storm," I said, although I used the correct lyrics with Cyn.

"Been listening to your sappy station again, have we?"

"And why did they have two cats—why not two dogs in the yard? Why was he so happy Betty Lou was going out that night?"

"Write the story. Then you'll know why." After a few moments of reflecting, Cyndi said, "I want to know what Judy Garland thought in her last few minutes of life. I want to know if Marilyn really took her own life or if she was done in by the mob."

After she died I thought of this conversation many, many times. How could I have not paid better attention? If I had, would anything have changed? Cyn, what was your last thought?

Oh, Cyn. What if your only job in this world was to brighten up the day of people you came into contact with? And what if you did that very well, without even realizing it? You lit people up just by looking at them. You gave them hope just by being in their presence.

Yikes—the wave was engulfing again. It was so bad, I had to turn it off somehow. Couldn't I shift into overdrive with my work and workouts and auditions, if only just to ease the pain?

I did; it worked—for a little while. For a couple of weeks, I felt nothing, absolutely nothing. I trudged through day after day feeling....nothing. Nice try. One night I pulled the car over and leaned my head on the steering wheel and screamed. And screamed some more. And then I screamed some more. I screamed so much my face hurt. I had to hold my forehead to keep it from creasing, it hurt so much. This was way beyond an ugly cry. This was monstrous.

Cyn. Oh, CynCynCynCynCynCynCynCynCyn.

Some part of my brain started lecturing the screaming part. This is dreadful. But I am not. This is the worst. I am good. This is unbearable. But I can bear it. Somehow. "Oh, shut up and let me scream!" I screamed.

I love my family, but it's a dutiful love. I've loved boyfriends, but nothing ever came close to this.

CynCynCynCynCynCynCynCynCyn.

Cyn, I had no idea you were so everything to me. You were my favorite person on this entire planet. What would you have done if I'd ever said any of the things I regret not saying to you? Would you have done anything different? But I did say a few things. I told you not to eat garbage—it makes you feel like garbage. I told you not to drink and do pills. I told you to love yourself almost as many times as you told me to love myself. I suggested we both quit this crazy business and do something easy and soothing. Move to Venice Beach and work in a little tchotchke stall. Move to Florida and work in a greenhouse. Move to Maui and work in a surf shop. Life doesn't have to be as hard as we were making it.

Remember that one gal I told you about, the one who came to LA, had one audition, and went home? Sometimes I envied her and wished beyond all get-out that I'd done that. No, life didn't have to be as hard as we'd been making it.

Truthfully, I envy easily. I drive by a couple unpacking their car and obviously settling in for the night, and I want to be them. And when I'm in my house and I see a fun car loaded down with surfboards, I want to be free and playful like them. When I lived in an apartment, I yearned for a house with a yard. I'd live in a house with a yard, and sometimes I'd want the ease and simplicity and freedom of living in an apartment. I stare at a picture and want to be there, experiencing that. Then I'm there, experiencing that, and I want to go home to my palm trees. I see a successful actor and I'd want to be her—oh, the lights, the glamour. I'd see a salesclerk in a convenience store, and I'd want to be her—oh, the simplicity, the far fewer expectations. I was FOMO before it was a thing. (For those peeps thirty years in the future, FOMO is the feeling of missing out.)

I always wanted to be wherever I wasn't…except when I didn't.

After that ceerrrrraaaaarazy cry, and totally thankful that a cop didn't stop to see what was up—or down, as the case was—with me, I drove home. Well, okay, I got it out of my system, I thought. I felt so much lighter, like a clear, blue sky after an earth-shattering, body-shaking Wisconsin thunderstorm. I can't imagine anything else being in there. Maybe I can move ahead with my life now.

Ha! Grief doesn't work quite that way. It came back. And then came back again. And then again.

At least I had my palm trees. I'm very possessive of them, as you can see.

For the first time ever, I didn't care about who was nominated for a Golden Globe. Some actor friends invited me to a watch party, but I couldn't go. I started to watch the show by myself, snuggled into one of the big chairs, but turned it off.

Something made me walk into Cyn's old room. I hadn't been in there since that woman cleared it out, although the housekeeper goes in there. Cyn was still in there. She was still everywhere, really. Don't we move on after we leave here? How could she be starting her next journey and still…be *so* here?

I wandered back into the living room and turned the Golden Globes back on. I really didn't feel like I was watching them alone in the room. Great...now I'm completely losing it, I thought.

Action! Camera! Lights!

Cara got me an audition for a pretty decent part, and I nailed it—a down-on-her-luck waitperson who helps the lead character find her life. Bah! I failed miserably at doing that for my friend, but at least I could do it in a movie that millions of people would see. This movie, too, was filming right away, thankfully. Months can often pass between auditions and film shoots.

This was another supporting role, but the movie had name actors in it. Possibly because I was hanging out with well-known stars, the crew treated me differently this time, a little...fawningish, like lots of little fanboys. I found it annoying.

One time Cyn came in and plopped her five-foot-six-inches of ooziness onto the sofa.

"How are you doing?" I asked.

"Fine."

You know that kind of *fine*...when someone's definition of fine has settled into something less agreeable than s/he'd like.

"I believe you."

"I wanted this my whole life, and I almost can't stand it."

"What?"

"Not what, who. Them. The people. The bloodsuckers, the parasites. It's like they're feeding on me."

"They're not really parasites. They're more like moths who are attracted to your flame."

"Let them find their own flame."

"They will."

"But in the meantime, they're feeding on me."

"So? Let them. They can't really take anything from you. Give it away. Lavish it on them. More will come back to you, and it might even help them find their own light faster."

The Alcoholics Anonymous folks say that the reason the program works is that we humans are not all crazy at the same time. We're all so wise for each other. We really do know stuff. We're so wise to ourselves, too, but sometimes it's more often for another. That's why we have each other, why there are so many of us: to remind each other constantly, because we forget constantly. Cyn said another version of that conversation from the other side to me, more than once. I repeated my side, more than once, to her.

Back to the annoying, fawning crew...OMG, I realized we'd been doing it backwards. Cyndi and I wanted the glamour but not the stickiness. We can't have the glamour, though, until we can handle the stickiness—and for starters, reframing it away from stickiness and calling it something a little more loving would certainly help.

Something else shifted for me that day. You know how people, especially celebrities, walk around kind of on their guard like "Oh my God, what do these people want from me?" Not all celebrities do that, of course, but some do. Many fans are quite fickle and impossible to please, which can be crazymaking to people who rely on fans for their livelihood and success. Most people, even (especially?) the superstars, are deeply flawed. Fans love us to be strong—until they don't. Then they love us to be vulnerable—until they don't. People loved Princess Diana because she was strong yet vulnerable, beautiful yet bashful. Most of us in the public eye are happy to share our vulnerabilities...*after* we've made it out the other side of whatever it was we had to go through to make us the phenomenal person we now are. Breathe on nails, polish them on shirt.

Fans also want us contrite when we've done something wrong. They're quick to forgive transgressions, as long as they're not pervy (thank you—*not*—Kevin Spacey et al....

ceerrrrrrrrrrreeeeeeeeeeepy!!!) and as long as we're completely contrite.

So, what was the shift? I made the conscious decision to switch from "Here I am" to "There you are!" I turned internally asking "How can I lift you up today?" into my new hobby. Then the energy doesn't come *at* me, you, us—it goes *from* us. Don't put up a shield. Send out a ray of light!

I realized I'd stopped walking into an audition saying "Pleaseohpleaseohpleaseohplease give me this part." I just became the part. I don't walk into a cafe and try to shield myself from all the people who wonder what they've seen me in and want to bask in what they think is my beauty (you people did *not* see me when I woke up this morning, did you?!). No, they're basking in the light I'm suddenly not hoarding anymore.

Maybe I've been my biggest energy sucker.

The list of the Oscar nominees came out, and Cyn wasn't here to gripe over it.

"Are you kidding? She got nominated for that pitiful acting job?"

She wasn't her most gracious on that particular morning of the year. Neither was I, for that fact.

My favorite rendition of why the Oscars are called Oscars is that once-Academy president Bette Davis, it's been told, named the little statue after her husband's middle name. Cyn, who had a cousin Oscar, liked the version that one of the Academy's secretaries said it reminded her of her "Uncle Oscar," which was actually a pet name for a cousin.

Last year I summoned up some graciousness and said to Cyn, "You'll be on the list someday."

She burst into tears. "It's too late!"

How long had she been thinking about, well, leaving?

The Grammys came and went, and I didn't watch. That was one of our things, too.

Whimpersniffle.

Yeah, About That One, Too...I'm Not Sure Either

I headed to the beach, but rain started pelting the car. I pulled over on a turnout on one of my favorite roads in LA—Kanan Road from Highway 101 to Pacific Coast Highway. I often drove out of my way to take that route (and avoid the traffic through Malibu). I just sat and watched the rain hit the windshield. The drops would slowly merge together, bulge, and then quickly slip down the pane in one bigger drop conglomeration. That's probably what my teardrops were doing on my face, too. At least my forehead wasn't creasing in that painful way.

Why, why, why?

The rain didn't have much of a response to my question about how life could be so painful, but my mind started thinking of things. To keep the heart open? To love, no matter what? Maybe that's why, why, why.

I headed home and hit a traffic jam. People in LA forget how to drive when it rains. For once I just sat in the parking lot of a highway.

The traffic has become worse since I moved here. But it has in New York, Denver, San Francisco, every big city. Well, some places have no traffic, but they have hurricanes, tornadoes, or blizzards. Some have both traffic *and* wild weather. (Notice this isn't a book about one of those places?) We've gone from talking about traffic like it's a living, breathing, moving thing to talking about it like it's a clogging, artery-blocking, dying thing. We have glorious weather almost every day of the year, yes, but, also yes, we have this traffic, too. As I mentioned earlier, I seldom have to deal with it, but when I do, I'm grateful that those times are rare. The times I find myself stuck in a jam are usually due to an accident, and that can happen anywhere, and I usually get off at the next exit and go do something else for a while.

A friend of mine once mentioned how she was standing in one of the big New York City train stations; she felt like she was in one of those scenes from a movie where she was standing still and everyone else was rushing by at the speed of light. It was crazymaking AF. (That's As Fuck, for the people reading this in thirty years.) She said she'd take LA traffic over that any day of the week and twice on Sundays. At least we're in our cars learning a new language or dictating letters or something productive....like crying over love songs.

When I'm not listening to my sappy love-song station, which is mostly at night, or NPR, which is mostly mid-day, I drive around listening to the Beach Boys a lot. Shhhhhhhh—don't tell anyone! That is just so not cool. Actually, my mother gave me this thing I have about the Beach Boys. She played them a lot when I was little. She really loved them, which I found rather strange for a Wisconsin farmgirl. She played a lot of music from the 'fifties and 'sixties as I was growing up, mostly while she'd clean the house (or try, anyway). She was listening to that music while I was watching movies from that era...and before that era...and after that era.

I read a line in a book once where the author reminisced about growing up in LA and stated that life was in the "sweet refrains of the Beach Boys and we would scoop it up like ice cream." Something like that. In Wisconsin it was more like the tooth-hurting, ear-grating, soul-jarring screech of the factories, and we would chew on it like a hunk of cheese sausage and swig beer.

Truthfully, I can't stand even the smell of beer, and, okay, that's so not fair. Wisconsin has many very, very beautiful parts. My favorite part of the state is up in Door County, where we used to go camping by the lake. Along with Christmas, those were my favorite times of my childhood. I heard a piece on NPR about how Americans love their lakes, and a fair number of folks called in with fond memories of their summers by some odd lake or another. I almost called in to rave about my lake.

Almost Every Good Thing I Ever Learned about Life I Learned from Improv

Well, I absolutely had to do something fun. Improv was something fun. I'd taken scads of classes years earlier, and found I was quite good at it. I started performing with a team, but eventually felt it was taking too much time away from preparing for auditions and the other highlights of trying to make it in this town.

I looked up a few members of my old team on Facebook and saw that they were still performing somewhat regularly at a comedy club in the Valley.

"Hell, yeah!" they replied when I asked if I could join them again.

OMG! Rehearsals were so much fun and made me forget about the rest of my life (read: Cyn) for a little bit.

The title of this section actually nails it. For instance, if you're in the middle of a scene and you find you're not having fun, if you're just looking for an out, ask what could make this fun? At the time I was taking improv I was involved in a bunch of day jobs that weren't really floating my boat much. One day, instead of just wishing the hours would pass more quickly, I thought how could I make this more fun? Well, music was first on the list, so I turned on Pandora. Straightening out my desk and making my work area feel homier was second on the list. Writing out an intention helped. And...and...and....

The primary job of anyone in improv is to say, "Yes, and...." I hadn't realized how contrary and full of "No, but..." I was until I started doing improv. Unlike the opposite of the valley of the happy people for screenplays, improv doesn't thrive on conflict but on teasing each other to create a world that'd never been even conceived before. Like books and movies, audiences will believe any world you create for them, as long as you set up the scene to be (for example) on Alpha Centauri from the beginning, or near it, at least. Some mystery can be there. But you can't spring it on them at the end—audiences don't like that.

I soon learned that I did a crazy thing: when someone threw a line at me, I'd try to throw it back as quickly as possible...like I didn't deserve to hold onto it or something cuckoo like that. "Slow down and take up space and time," a teacher once told me in private. "You deserve it." I went home and cried.

Some more great points: Talking is the least important form of communication. It's never about the joke; it's about being real, and the humor regarding whatever aspect of the human condition that's front and center makes itself known. Before every show we'd pat each other on the back, saying, "I got your back." It's such a team sport. A huge emphasis is on making each other look good—no one wants to play with someone who doesn't care about them. Wow, can you imagine how different life would be if the focus was on making each other look good, not trying to outshine anyone else? Maybe the NMPOTUS should take up improv.

I could write a whole book about improv—all the games we play, all the different forms we do. Suffice it to say that improv is unlike 'most anything else...it's basically about saying yes to the gift offered in each moment. It's also like going to camp and just having the biggest blast with really fun folks.

"Hey, Trish! How've you been?"

"You kind of disappeared off Facebook. It's good to see you're doing well."

"What have you been up to?"

"Oh, you know—getting ever closer to that star on the Hollywood Walk of Fame."

I couldn't tell them yet. I wanted to take full advantage of the fact that not only was improv fun, but also that this particular group hadn't been friends with Cyn. I didn't want that watchful eye on me that my other groups of friends had. I didn't mean to be dishonest, but for a while I needed a place to go where Cyn's suicide didn't have to be a something. I'd tell them sometime. In the meantime, oh! It was such a great relief to be there.

But driving home, of course, I'd remember. Cyn never did improv; she did stand-up from time to time. Oh, she was funny. Robin Williams was her major hero, other than her dad and John Wayne. Note to self: about those heroes we choose....

Well, I've heard that Robin had a terrible neurological disease. I had to watch someone I loved to the moon and back slowly die from such a disease. I'd choose Robin's way any day.

Rehearsals took place at night, so of course I was listening to love songs on my way home. I still translated everything into Cyn. I loved your imperfections that were oh, so perfect (thanks, John), Cyn—as much as you loved mine.

One particular imperfection made us fight like an old, married couple, though—a miserable, old, cranky married couple at that. Maybe this comes from being of hearty Midwestern stock, but I love chores. I know—crazy. But they're peaceful and calming, and I love the routine. Cyn, not so much. While I love chores, however, I didn't love doing them for someone else.

"Stop leaving a mess everywhere you go!"

"Get a life!"

We finally hired a housekeeper and that ended the quarreling about chores. But then I didn't have the peace and calm from my chore routine. So then we fired the housekeeper, and I did the inside chores and Cyn did the outside chores, since she found peace and calm in weeding...until she didn't anymore, so that didn't work anymore, and we hired another housekeeper and gardener.

I loved our (my, I guess) most recent housekeeper—*loved* her. I didn't want to let her go, either, so I kept her on, even though I could've easily done the chores myself. I never really knew the gardener, though, since Cyn dealt with him. I kept him on just for mowing and I took to weeding—just for something real to be doing.

The radio switched from John to Sam. Cyn, why didn't you stay? With me, that is. (It's hard to go Yoda on that particular line—too short.)

Good thing I'm not in a relationship, I thought. After pining for one all of my adult life, even when I was in one, I figured that was about the last thing I could've handled right then.

CHAPTER 6

Cue the Crazy Guy and Malibu Ken

There's this crazy guy. He has a crazy old mansion in the Hollywood Hills chockablock with movie memorabilia, leftover items from movie sets, and other oddments he's collected from around town. Chockablock is being polite—crammed, overflowing, up to the rafters would be more accurate.

I have been to so many wrap and opening-night parties at houses up in them thar, or these here, really, hills. There was one movie I wasn't even in, but I was some crew guy's arm ornament. The film was about the Armenian genocide and so the party celebrated Armenian culture, Armenian food, Armenian dancing, Armenian everything. "They tried to silence us a century ago," the director said, "but it didn't work. We're still here and we're still dancing."

The movie was extremely powerful, and it's times like those that I absolutely adore and appreciate this industry for the influential messages it can convey. Movies can change lives. So can speeches, politics, and books, of course. So can quiet people just lighting up their neighborhoods. My chosen vehicle is movies. Being in gorgeous mansions with that amazing view of the Hollywood lights and with the yummiest gourmet finger foods doesn't hurt either.

Although it came with that view and the yummy food, Claude's was unlike any other house in the hills, however. A full-size statue of Goofy greets every guest. A knight in armor stands guard in the massive living room, which is full of red-velvet furniture. Some of the beds in the bedrooms are round, with mirrors overhead. That all might be fun, but I heard it's terrible feng shui. Well, so is clutter. As various up-and-coming bands would play on the patio, I watched the Hollywood lights twinkle in the not-too-distant distance.

Once I was in the bathroom, and I looked up to find a creepy clown grinning down on me from the skylight. That was the night I met the guy with the foot fetish. I almost stopped going after that, but the insistent lure of finding things and people and situations and conversations you'd never find anywhere else was too much to resist.

I say Claude and his house are "crazy" with much affection. He isn't the insane kind of crazy, but the fun, wild, eccentric kind. I prefer crazy (well, this kind), really. He just doesn't conform to anyone else's idea of how a life should be lived. His long, wavy white hair flows down his back—kind of a symbol of someone who's seen so many ages come and go and has made his choice to keep one particular age in the present. Hey, I wonder if he knows Skye. I want long, wavy white hair someday.

One time I stayed really, really late talking to some fascinating person or other and ended up falling asleep on the couch in...the Jungle Room, I believe it was, complete with palm trees, wallpaper with a pattern of green bamboo, a (fake) leopard throw on the bed, and animal art all over. Claude had a number of different rooms with distinct motifs. I certainly wasn't alone; bunches of folks were strewn here and there all over the house in the various "rooms": the Queen's Room, the Red Room, the Hookah Room, the Game Room, and the Bed Room—as in a room that has just one giant bed.

At about five in the morning, I heard something that sounded like souls wailing at the gates of hell...if there was such a thing as hell with a gate and souls wailing there.

"What in creation is that?" I mumbled.

"Coyotes," someone answered. Ohhhhkay then!

Cyndi and I went to a *lot* of parties there. It was hard to even think of going back after Cyn died. She was my crazy-guy-crazy-house compadre. I didn't know how I'd do it without her. So I didn't.

But not long after my meltdown in the car, I received an email from my wonderfully crazy friend announcing a South Seas Valentine's Day party. I forced myself into the car, then forced myself down the road, then forced myself onto the freeway, then forced myself up his road, then forced myself to walk into his house after sitting in the car for an hour or so plotting my escape.

I slowly made my way through the jumble of garden gnomes and Goddess statues in the courtyard and into the front room. With its dark wood paneling, the room was dark even at high noon, let alone at midnight. Lamps lit up the corners. Someone was playing the piano, as someone always was—sometimes a famous musician, sometimes not.

"Patricia?"

I turned around but didn't see anyone I recognized. I started heading out of the room.

"Patricia?"

I turned around again. By this time almost everyone in the little room was looking at me, so I couldn't tell who had called my name.

And in between the couple making love on the tiny sofa (it gets way cray at Claude's) and the requisite stares-through-narrowed-eyes-and-looks-oh-so-infinitely-wise-but-never-says-anything guy, there he was. A man with wavy, brown hair and warm, brown eyes moved over on a little bench and patted the spot next to him. I had absolutely no idea who he was, but there was something quite compelling about the gentleness in his eyes. Besides, I needed a break from trying to step over stuff and people.

"You don't remember me, huh?" he asked after I sat down.

"I'm sorry, I don't. Was it from a movie?"

"No. High school back in Packers Country."

Now that was really weird. My high school was pretty small, and everyone knew everyone. I looked at him.

"I look a little different."

AWKward! Oh, great. He was a female back then—which is fine if he was; it just makes the guessing that much harder.

"Jeff." And when I still didn't respond, he added, "Harding."

SUper awkward! Jeff Harding? Who the hell—

"Jeff! It's so nice to see you again."

He smiled, clearly acknowledging that he knew I was doing the LA-BS thing.

"What brings you to LA?" I asked, trying to change the tone from the LA-BS thing—and failing miserably, I was sure. "And Claude's house in particular?"

"Well, what brought me to LA was college nineteen years ago, and then I stayed."

College nineteen years ago. "As a freshman?"

"Yes."

So that'd make him a couple years younger. Well, all right then—I can ease up on my guilt a little bit; seniors in high school don't really know the ones following as well as the ones they were following.

"It's okay," he said. "I don't expect you to remember me. Want to get something to drink?"

"Sure. By the way, I go by Trish now."

"Oh, sorry."

"No problem."

We wandered through the kitchen and into the dining room where we opened the bottle of wine I brought. Then we wandered up the stairs to a rooftop patio where we sat among palm trees lit up by little flood lamps. A woman in full mermaid frippery hopped by (well, she couldn't exactly walk), followed by another woman decked out as an alien Morticia. At a South Seas party? Maybe she'd been looking at an old invitation. Or maybe she was just doing her own thing.

Claude had his usual harem (male and female) around him. I caught his eye, and his spark of joy at seeing me was quickly overshadowed by the sadness at not seeing Cyn. He'd always had a thing for her. He started to move in my direction, but half a dozen revelers suddenly swept him downstairs and out to the pool area. It was just as well…I couldn't handle his pain right now.

No one really knows what Claude does. Just tending to his house and his eccentricities and his people seems to be a fulltime occupation.

"Where do you work?" I asked this mysterious younger man.

"*LA Times.*"

Great—he probably works in the movie review section, and he's the one who panned the zombie flick.

"Sports, mostly."

Ugh. As much as I love working out and being physical, some organized sports are akin to gladiator games to me.

"Football?" I asked.

"Tennis and golf and things like that."

Phew!

A couple in full pirate regalia walked by, followed by someone done up as a starfish. Truth be told, I'd missed Claude's. When I went to his parties, there was nowhere else on Earth I'd rather be. They were (and still are) beyond enthralling.

"I saw you at the beach a few weeks ago."

"Ohhhhhhh, right!"

His smile let me know he was ignoring my LA-BS thing again. "But I got a call that an interview I'd been waiting and waiting for was finally going to happen."

Ohhhh, *that* guy. "Great!"

"You looked like you'd rather have been alone anyway. And I knew I'd see you again. I actually see you a lot."

I didn't want to continue the LA-BS thing, so I wracked my brain for something logical to say. "I.....I don't know what to say." That was logical—not.

"It's okay," he said. "Sometimes that's the best thing to say."

"Where do you see me?"

"Here. There. Everywhere. I guess I still have the habit of not talking to seniors when I was a sophomore." We laughed. "I was married to an actor for a bit," he continued.

"Oh, that must've been.....interesting." I chuckled. "Glad you're free of that?"

It was his turn to chuckle. "The being an actor wasn't the bad part. She actually got some decent TV roles, so she was happy about that. Some people just don't want to be married is all." He was quiet for a few seconds while he avoided me looking at him. Then he chuckled again. "When I mention I've been married, women always look at me like I've been housebroken."

"I must still be an untrained pup in that regard, then." I laughed and laughed. And laughed. And laughed. The laughter turned into sobs—raucous, hiccuppy, gasping-for-breath sobs. He put his arm around me and held me.

"My best friend killed herself. This was one of our most favorite places to come to together."

"I'm so sorry."

"Talk about being ghosted. I didn't see that one coming. Psych!" I was babbling; at least the hiccu-gasp sobs had subsided.

"Uh, that's not exactly what ghosting—"

"I know," I howled. The sobs started up again, as did the babbling at the same time. "You know the thing about being ghosted? Ghosts are amazingly powerful." The sobs won out over the babbling. Jeff held my hand for a couple minutes while I tried not to make a scene. At Claude's, though, it's very easy not to be the one making the scene as so many scenes are unfolding all over his house and property all the time.

"I'm so, so sorry," Jeff said when my sobs subsided again.

"I'm sorry, too—I have to go."

Another cry, even more monstrous than that monstrous-to-beat-all-monstrous ones, came two blocks away from the party. It exhausted me, and I obviously fell asleep for a few hours because I woke up to a gorgeous sunrise. I started the car and headed home.

Home. I'd started to dread going home. Looking back, I probably should've moved out right away, but back then I just couldn't bear to lose another precious thing in my life.

We Really Can't "Go Home" Anymore...Not That I Wanted To

As chance would have it, I was heading back to the Dairy State a few days later for my annual pilgrimage. I never "book out" when I go out of town, as long as the trip is within the North American borders, if there's the slightest chance I could board a plane to LA and be there within six hours for that all-important, life-changing audition. For twenty-two years, I've been almost always available to be "on avail" for a role.

As soon as I got to my old room, still somewhat as I left it (perhaps Mom wanted to conduct tours as soon as I finally made it big), I opened my high-school yearbook and looked for the class a couple years behind mine.

Jeffrey Harding....hmmmmm....oh, there he was. Well, no wonder I didn't recognize him: he'd certainly filled out—big time, in the good way—from the geeky pip-squeak he was back then. I'd started to blossom by the time my senior pic was taken, but I wouldn't dare look at my earlier high-school yearbooks. Blossoming wasn't even a far-off fantasy in those years.....I didn't think it'd ever be for me.

And judging from the melancholy look on Jeff's face staring up at me from the page, he obviously didn't think it'd ever be for him, either. But it was. Big time.

He also had some really, really strange hair happening back then, back there. It's almost as if he went from a troll to Malibu Ken with a good dose of adorable Teddy Bear thrown in. The long-haired, fuzzy-headed kind of troll, I mean, not the Internet kind.

I didn't find it all that strange that he and I met so far from home. LA is a magnet. A bunch of us from my hometown ended up here. What would've been even stranger was if we'd all ended up in Lodi or Topeka together.

Yoda laughed from my phone, which alerted me that I'd received a text. No matter what state of mind I'm in, Yoda's laugh always (well, the last ten months not so much) makes me smile.

"Want 2 go 4 a walk @ beach? This is Jeff, BTW," read the text. When did I give him my number? Oh, right—I vaguely remembered slipping him a card as I dashed from the party. That was certainly an...........interesting thing for me to do.

"Closest beach 2 me now is @ Lake Michigan."

"(Surprised emoji.) OK. It can wait until you're back. Say hi to my mom for me, LOL."

"LOL. I'll b bk @wkend. Walk then?"

Mom dragged me off to one of her craft fairs. I drove, as I do whenever I'm with her (except for that time right after Cyn died). The fair was one-hundred percent women and ninety-nine percent of them were overweight, usually very. I went without makeup and with my hair up in a ponytail, trying to blend in and feel more real. Even so, people would look at me as if they recognized me—"Who are you?" their eyes asked. "You look familiar. Where have I seen you?" That was kind of new.

Well, if you were up late for some really awful zombie flick, you would've seen me. I really don't regret the zombie show, though—it's still paying for some of my life these days, all these years later.

It's so strange to live in a land of beautiful people. A large part of the acting world (minus the character actors) are often the best-looking people from any given town. The Olympics have the best athlete from a given town. MIT has the best geek from a given town (and I say that with the utmost respect for geeks). Looks are one of LA's prime commodities.

But...one thing my hometown folks seemed to have, in addition to clogged arteries, probably and unfortunately, was...contentment. Ease with what is. No angst over what's supposed to be. No constant striving. They were... smiling! Not...posing! Most people in LA need something. It gets very enervating. If it's not a role or a job someone needs, it's a partner, or a boost of inspiration, or a new group of friends because they've outgrown the old ones.

Many folks don't understand how people can drop their friends so easily as they're moving up whatever ladder. I do...I mean I understand, although I try not to drop my old friends. And it's not easy. But the old friends remember us how we were and often expect us to stay that way. The new ones welcome who we are in that moment. The old ones might mean well, but comments like "Must be nice!" or "Don't forget us little people!" get old.

Many of my more successful LA friends say that high-school reunions are just those couple of comments over and over. I always figured my reunions would be more of the why-haven't-you-made-it-yet routine, so I avoided them. The wistful stuff comes from earlier LA friends who are still Ubering and catering, and it's understandable, but it can feel cumbersome, weighty, wearing. If we love these folks enough, we can tolerate it. If we don't, there's no point.

Some friends can travel the whole, long road with us, but they are rare. Oh, Cyn. My heart panged as I watched early-forty-something besties or sisters walk together.

Come to think of it, she was taking up more space in my life in her death than she did beforehand—and she took up a lot of space then. Crazy, friggin' friend! I don't mean to sound flippant about it, but sometimes I was just so freaking angry I could've killed her. Some days I was just in a rage that she was gone, that she put me through this, that I couldn't even talk to her about this, that I had no say in when our friendship would be over and I was far from done with her, and it just sucked and was fucking awful. And seeing besties laughing together didn't help.

I didn't hold on to any of my friends from Wisconsin. Remember Jenni, my best friend whom I couldn't stand? We bumped into her at the fair. OMG, she'd gained about two hundred pounds. The only way I recognized this stranger who called out to me was when she smiled—then the old Jenni came into view.

"How are you?" she gushed.

"Good, good. How about you?"

"Oh, good. You know, just doing the doing-the-life thing."

Well, that was a whole lot more than I could say about one of my friends.

But that was about it—that was all Jenni and I had to say to each other. She had two darling daughters in tow. They were her thirty years ago—long blonde hair, big blue eyes, copping an attitude already. But she had little beings in her life, like I was suddenly intensely longing for. She looked a little wistful at my carefree (ha!) existence. What was it about that grass and it being ever so greener...anywhere we're not?

I didn't text Jeff when I got back. I decided I couldn't take seeing him after my meltdown at Claude's house.

Oh, well. Journalists aren't known for their depth and spirituality anyway. Actually, neither are actors. But we can be quite surprising in that regard. Maybe he'd surprise me.

What really surprised me was I was looking for depth and spirituality.

This Happened (people thirty years from now—this phrase was a thing)

I said that Christmas sucks when you're single...*and* your BFF killed herself. So do Sunday mornings. And Sunday afternoons. And Sunday nights.

Unless I'm in a movie, Sundays aren't that different from Mondays. It's just the whole idea of it.

I'd get up and get dressed and go to my spiritual center, but even that didn't get me out of my funk.

It's called grief, Trish. And you're allowed to have it.

I used to drag—I mean take—Cyndi to my gym on Sunday afternoons. It wasn't as crowded then, because regular people go to the beach on Sundays. Actors go to the beach on weekdays, when they're not so crowded. I mentioned that she'd let me help her with her workouts, but not so much on Sundays, when she'd want to lounge. But we'd go because we were single and Sundays are family days, and we didn't want to hang out at the house, which Sunday blared, "I just want to get in your face that this place is so totally without a family!" Nor did we want to go to places families frequent, like...most places on Sundays, or so it seemed.

I was once trying to show Cyn how to lift weights really, really slowly. "Okay, count how long it takes me to lift this."

"One chimpanzee, two chimpanzee—"

So much for that set. We burst into hysterics. She made everything fun. Everything.

I tried looking for fun elsewhere. I tried having lunch with girlfriends, but they'd still be searching my face for clues to how as I was doing and perhaps trying to ascertain that I wouldn't think of doing what Cyndi did... would I?

Cyndi was like my softest, comfiest, most treasured sweater, and I didn't want to wear any others. I didn't mean to withdraw from my peeps, but...I was.

"Honey, you're being alone too much," Cara gently scolded.

"I'm just catching up on all the TV serials and binge watching the hot shows, is all."

"Nice try. When's the last time you did something really fun?"

"Improv rehearsal last week."

"What else?"

"I went to the beach yesterday."

"By yourself?"

"Yes."

"Honey, when's the last time you fucked a man?" Cara could talk like a trucker when she wanted to get a point across. We haven't even talked about swearing. I don't, generally, which is an extremely rare commodity in this town. A friend of mine once said that swearing makes you common, and ever since I heard that, if I ever swear, it must be a really rough situation. You've heard me swear; it's been a really rough situation.

"I don't remember," I said.

"I don't remember," I said to Cyndi once, referring to something or other.

"Oh, yes, you do. You remember everything I've ever said or done for the entire twenty years we've known each other."

We laughed and laughed. I laughed and laughed at the memory until I started crying.

She was right. I had a habit of remembering....too much, really—usually, anyway. It was just how my brain functioned.

Grief paints such vivid pictures that it's easy to remember things. But I shut a lot of pictures down when

Brian died—I just couldn't bear it. Who could blame me, though? I was nine!

I found myself thinking of Brian a lot. What was that— his way-too-short lifetime—all about? Why? How could Life create such a beautiful, loving child, only to take him decades, almost a whole lifetime, too early? Why are so many people born with disabilities? Why, why, why? What a crazy, messed-up world this can be.

Maybe the experience of losing Bri could've opened my heart. Instead, it closed it, as twenty-twenty hindsight was telling me. Bri. Cyn.

I cried...and then cried some more.....and then cried some more...and then did it all over again.

Perhaps Cyndi—or, more accurately, the sudden lack of Cyndi—opened my heart again. Epic.

A Kitchen Comeback

I told you I was a foodie and even a gourmet cook years before, but living with Cyndi made me practically forget I'd ever held a potholder. She didn't cook at all, and I never felt comfortable cooking in what was her kitchen, after all. She made me feel at home everywhere else in the house, but not there. I got used to making just my morning smoothies and frequenting the prepared-food section of Whole Foods.

Over the months since she made her grand exit, I'd make forays through the kitchen cabinets, but it didn't feel good, like I was betraying her. It was kind of like visiting a museum of a very strange culture, too. What are all these gadgets and things? A can-opener—really? A.... what the hell is this thing? Oh, a potato/French fry cutter.

The counters were so barren, but I didn't want to just fill them up with blenders and mixers and stuff like that. I actually went online and looked at kitchen setups to get inspired. Some foodie I am, I thought. Oh, well. Just out of practice, I figured.

"Alrighty then, that's a start," I said to myself as I put a vase for fresh flowers, some glass canisters full of interesting-looking grains, and a jar of garlic and sundried tomatoes in olive oil in my grocery cart. Actually, I might've said it a little more loudly than I thought because the other people in the kitchen-stuff aisle at the store looked at me funny. I miss having someone to talk to all the time.

After the gym that Sunday, I went to Whole Foods to buy a bunch of ingredients to make soup and a casserole. OMG, it was so good, if I did say so myself. Cooking can be so soothing....and time consuming.

C'mon Monday—get here already fer cryin' out loud... which I did.

CHAPTER 7

"Oh, Grow Up!"

some old geezer once reprimanded me.

Grow up. *Grow up*? Hmmmm, grow up. I could tell from his particular parlance that he meant to grow up and put childish dreams behind me and go get a real job. But grow up. Grow *up*. Isn't growing up being the person who can achieve wild dreams? Isn't growing up, growing *upward*—like a vine can grow up the wall—and not just older, not even just more mature, as I'm sure the man was implying?

But was I supposed to give up on the dream? What if I packed my bags and left five minutes before the call that'd change everything? Unlike *Lala Land*, I didn't always necessarily have a man in my life who'd come after me to let me know that a major casting director wanted to see me.

But then was holding on to the dream of that call magical thinking? Or was it holding true to my dreams? Or....

Isn't it enough to want something with all your heart? Isn't it enough to hang in there year after year, keeping a great attitude and not giving up? Or....

Maybe we can't get it wrong, I thought in one of my rare moments when I wasn't feeling like a sponge that'd been wrung out way too many times. Whatever we do..... here we are. Loving, living, laughing, learning—no matter what we're doing, those things don't have to stop. And everything we do leads us...somewhere.

I once read an article about Condoleezza Rice, which said that when folks would ask her how she got to where she was, she'd say something along the lines of, "Well, first you fail at being a piano major." How crazy great is that? She loved playing the piano, obviously, but her soul had other plans. Maybe the piano just kept her busy and happy while her being was being sculpted into being a person who could be Secretary of State. (Lots of being in there!)

And that old dude who told me to grow up? He probably gave up his dream too soon and always regretted it. People can turn into pickles when their creative juices are not allowed to flow. We can always tell the ones who've soured—they're the ones who are discouraging us. And me pursuing my dreams might've made him sad, but it's easier to be mad than sad. He actually wasn't all that old age-wise—just way old before his time. Giving up the dream can do that to people.

The thing about dreams is to have the essentials covered. Then we never have to give up.

I was starting to wear down, though. I was so lonely for people, but people were the last thing I wanted to be around. Cara, Skye, my improv team, and the odd casting director and her little gaggle of helpers were the only exceptions.

There were days—weeks, in fact—when blissful denial would kick in and I'd get a lot done. I'd help Skye, run errands, and go to a bunch of auditions. I started teaching a couple of Zumba classes at the gym. I even got another client, a friend of Skye's. But soon exhaustion overwhelmed me.

Human beings actually need to be in a fair amount of denial just to make it through the day around here— meaning on this planet. If we really saw the destruction we do with so many of our choices, we'd go crazy. But we do need to see how we're destroying the planet, killing someone's spirit with a snide remark, seeing our best friend contemplate suicide right in front of us.

And when the shroud of denial comes off, we can also see what we're supposed to do—buy a hybrid, don't say that snide remark, save our best friend from her thoughts and herself.

Oh, that. Will I ever get over this? Will I ever forgive myself?

I can't imagine being a young, working mother and having my spouse killed in Afghanistan or Iraq or anywhere, really. Still having to take care of the kids and go to a fulltime job while dealing with pain that must be worse than this—oh, it was inconceivable. But.....at least she had kids. Sometimes my heart would ache and my clock would tick loudly over that little part of life that I'd skipped for some reason. Why? How did that happen? I'd always wanted children.

Although it doesn't compare to losing a spouse or a child, what about the grief of never finding a partner? What about the grief of never having a child? What about the grief of not living the life you wanted? Sure, we can find other sources of joy, but the grief over what we've lost can still live way down inside there.

My grief for Cyndi brought up every dredge of grief about every fucking mistake I've ever made in this miserable life of mine. Okay, that was just some days. Thankfully, it wasn't every day. And on the days my mind wasn't being my best friend, I'd take Cara out to lunch or stay in her office and eat peanut butter on crackers with her. She gave—and still gives—the best pep talks.

"Go to Paris, get swept off your feet, and come back well fucked and married."

Okay, some of her pep talks were better than others.

Married. That seems so far away that it'd be on the other side of forever. And....we can't just get married to check it off our to-do list, can we? I remember a friend of mine saying that as she was about to walk down the aisle, her only thought was, "How can I get out of this without making a scene?" For some reason, her thought had a big impact on me. She didn't get out of it then, but she did a few years later. Maybe I always figured I'd just cut to the few years later part.

And the Winner Is....

I actually went to an Oscars party. For the first time in decades, I hadn't seen all of the movies (which, in normal years, I watch long before the list even comes out), so I didn't know what movies to root for. My friends doted on me—making sure my wineglass was full, making sure I had food nearby, making sure someone was always by my side. Finally, they probably thought, back among the living.

Welllllll...almost.

Another role came my way. This time it was a star-crossed, lonely schoolteacher who ended up saving the day by diverting a student from blowing up the school. It was another right-away job; the woman who was supposed to play the part had become pregnant and was showing too much by the time filming rolled around—luckily for this last-minute replacement known as yours truly. We filmed over two weekends in a school.

Here I'm two-thirds done babbling and rambling to you and I haven't even talked about the actual art of making a movie. The process of filming is kind of crazy-making for people like me who tend to be linear thinkers (except when I'm not...which, come to think of it, is probably more often). The ever-patient crew sets up the lights and camera on one side of the set-up scene. After about a thousand hours of taping the cords down so no one breaks a neck, getting the lighting just so and the camera dollies just right, checking the boom stick with the mic on it along with the sound levels, and doing this and that and the other thing that requires phenomenal attention to the most infinitesimal of details, the actors come out and the director calls for from one to three dozen (not kidding) takes of the scene. One or more actors have their backs to the camera. Then the actors disappear and the ever-patient crew sets up the lights and camera from the other side. The actors who'd been facing the camera now have their backs to it, and the director calls for one to three dozen takes, focusing on the heretofore unseen actors. A few more shots are taken from above, from below, and maybe from inside the refrigerator or teapot (thank you, *Phantom Thread*) or from outside the window or something like that.

Sometimes the director or someone else reads the lines of the actors who aren't seen, so those actors can take a break. My favorite story about this kind of thing was how Francis Ford Coppola got Martin Sheen to wail for his meltdown scene in *Apocalypse Now*....They'd been filming (and filming and filming) overseas and Francis listed, one by one, many of the comforts Martin would've been missing from back home. I'd wail, too!

The linear part of me would make a great continuity person—the one who watches closely to make sure the actor picks up the water glass with the right hand in each take, not the left. Or she's always holding her fork in her left hand. Or the ketchup is put back in the same place each time. (Don't even get me started on *Pulp Fiction* in the continuity department!)

So...so much for the exciting world of being a movie star—being on set can be pretty boring much of the time. Hours and hours can go into a few minutes of actual filming. Those few minutes make those hours all worthwhile, though. Good books help.

The eating part can be big fun, too; the big studios feed us like royalty. There's a buffet banquet of bagels, scrambled eggs, appetizers, salads, casseroles, smoked salmon, and desserts, plus a coffee bar (to keep us awake on those late nights). The return on investment can be quite high, I'm sure: the more well fed the actors and crew are, the happier everyone is, and the better the movie might turn out.

Whenever I have access to a trailer, I eat in there, but I'm just as happy eating with the extras and the best boys (the assistant to the gaffer, who is the head of the electricians; another best boy is the assistant to the key grip, who's the head of the lighting and rigging folks... just in case you ever wondered about that). I've never had my own trailer, but I've shared one with women performing similar roles to mine.

Sitting in the editing bay isn't much better—for me it's like watching paint dry. Those folks have the patience of Job, watching the same clip over and over to get the right look, the right intonation, the right feel. It's a very good thing we all enjoy vastly different activities.

The super fun part is opening night...when those thousands upon thousands of hours—from the very first jotting of an idea in a notebook to the last bit of music over the final credits—all comes together. The theater darkens and the music swells and my heart is in ecstasy...at least until the movie gets panned the next day. Okay, that really only happened once, and while the zombie movie did get massively panned, it's still a lucky card in my life. Maybe the massive panning helped; maybe it encouraged people to go see what in the world could've possibly been so bad.

In the restroom I overheard the AD (assistant director) and the script woman talking really nasty about the director. They came in after I did, and although I was just about to flush, I just sat there while they did their business, talked even nastier, and finally left.

It doesn't even matter what they said, although I'll tell you that it was stupid—along the lines of....

"That imbecile doesn't know his ass from his elbow." Well, how illuminating is that?

"He should go back to nursery school and learn a different trade. Like ass-kissing and dick polishing."

"Or bending over more."

Yuck. Everyone's entitled to his or her opinion, of course. But this was just banal. I was a little older than these two, so I've probably seen at least as many directors in my time as they have. This director was pretty young (must've known someone somewhere), but I thought he was doing a good job.

After they left and I could finally leave, I overheard two actors talking about the lead in similar tones. Good gravy—find a better hobby, people.

Party On

There are some nasty, nasty people in this town. Well, maybe they're certainly not as nasty as that one producer I heard of who said, "Hold a gun to the guy's head," when he was trying to get an editor to finish…an animated film for children!

Oh, I suppose if I was going to be spiritually correct, I'd say there are some very confused people in this town. But they're nasty. Unkind. Outright mean. And……yes, they got confused along the way.

My chronic wet-noodle state made me…oh, I don't know…less patient…but perhaps wiser, too. On the drive home that night, I thought that the sooner people realize that everything they think and do comes back to them, the faster we'll all get there—wherever *there* is. The faster actors celebrate the success of others, the faster they'll be celebrating their own success.

Are you listening to yourself, Trish?

Oh……people can be……nasty. And that doesn't mean I was being nasty! (Although I can be in my moments, to be sure.) I remember telling a former friend that a former boss was very judgmental.

"She was just reflecting your own judgmentalism," he said.

"Oh, shut up," I didn't say out loud. No wonder he was always single. I actually deleted him from my contact list—something I rarely do.

We can see something in others that isn't necessarily our own issue. I get the "we're all one" thing and how everything is a reflection of us. But she was a bitch. I'm not a bitch, just....loopy.

Plus, I seem to attract crazies. One time I came home after being fired by this one nutjob of a boss. It wasn't the only time I had a crazy manager—I was a metal filing to their magnets for a while. She was certifiably crazy. Not long after I arrived in LA, I walked out of a job once, which was crazy stupid because I had absolutely no money and ended up sleeping on Cara's floor with a couple other actors who were between jobs, too.

And here was another crazy. Bottled misery, she was.

"Nothing she's ever done has been logical," Cyndi had said, "so why would you expect her to be logical now? Why would you be riled up by a decision she's made about...well, anything? Including, or especially about, you?"

This boss hated me. I couldn't do anything right in her eyes. Cyn helped me realize that I was valuing people's opinions about me even though I didn't value their opinions about much else. Why would I then take on their opinion about me as gospel?

Oh, the people in our lives and the places they take us—sometimes not necessarily places we wanted to go, either. One time I had a coworker who lifted my sights up to new dimensions and lifted my inner life up to heights I never thought I'd reach. But he wasn't particularly nice about it. A friend of mine has a term for such people who come into our lives and rearrange everything to be far better than it was before yet can be quite rude in their endeavors: ruthless angels.

Sometimes Cyn was mine and sometimes I was hers.

Rosanna Arquette made a documentary called *Searching for Debra Winger*. She interviewed a number of female actors about the trials and tribulations they face in carving out a career for themselves. It'd take a very different turn, I'm sure, in these post-Harvey Weinstein-exposed days. Harvey was far from the only sleazeball in town, of course. I didn't experience much actual harassment myself, probably because I was such small potatoes. Most of the casting directors are women, and I didn't hang much with many producers and directors, who are mostly men. But I did meet a bunch of horny guys who I would make quick excuses to and keep my distance from. Same went for Cyn, too. I guess we were lucky... here, anyway.

I said #metoo, too, though—I was groped in Italy once, plus an uncle was about to make a move on me at age twelve but my mom walked in, plus a few other things. Cyn experienced about the same amount of unpleasant stuff.

I had so many people—famous people, especially—on a pedestal. I had no idea what they were really going through. I felt so put-upon in this life I was living (but I was the one putting on most of the putting upon) and I truly thought 'most everyone else was just having a ball of a time. Oh, hey, look at Uma Thurman and Quentin Tarantino—they must be just reveling in this life of theirs, right? Uh, not so much, it turns out. Or at least it wasn't as much as I'd thought.

Those two and a whole lot more carry so much more than we ever know. We all do, really. I had a brilliant, highly talented artist friend whose mom used to bash him and throw him across the room in her alcoholic rages. These things we carry....

I had a coworker once who had a pretty happy, quiet life and she was about as deep as a puddle and as compassionate as a post. Tragedy struck her family and—not that I wish that on anyone, but it definitely seems to be one of the ways of this life—and she became, well, deep... maybe as deep as a well (ha! Okay, fine, something deeper) and as compassionate as a Buddhist nun.

Anyway, I'm babbling again. Back to Rosanna....She finally interviewed Debra, who had taken a hiatus from moviemaking. Debra said to Rosanna (I'm paraphrasing) not to base the value of her life on the parts she gets.

I mentioned that to Cyn one night when she was moping about not getting a role she'd auditioned for.

"Do you ever notice that you quote movies? Like.....all the fucking time?"

My fork stopped in midair halfway between my mouth and the Whole Foods deli box.

"Not just movies but TV shows, articles, songs. You quote them all the time."

Words fled from my brain. It was completely empty in there. I had no response.

"What would you say to me, just you, coming from you, not quoting anyone?"

Words were still lounging on a beach in a distant land somewhere, far from my brain and mouth.

"You're wise, you know," Cyn continued. "Tell me what you think—*you*, Trish. Not what Rosanna Arquette thinks or what Gloria Swanson said in *Sunset Boulevard* or anyone anywhere else."

A deafening silence filled the room. We both were quiet for quite a while, which was very unlike us.

I watched so many movies, read so many books and magazines, and heard so many songs, all from a very early age. They were one of my coping mechanisms, I guess. Who would I be without all that wisdom from all those sources? A fun, playful, talented, Mensa-qualified, hot babe, really, but, still......

"Give me some of you, drawing on your life," Cyn finally said. "Give me some of that. Tell me how to make my dreams comes true. Just you—not Michael Beckwith or Oprah or the Dalai Lama or anyone. You, Trish, tell me how it's done. How do we do this life thing we have here?"

The words boarded a jet plane and started flying back, albeit slowly. "Be crystal clear about what you want," I said. "Set the intention that what you want is here now. Give thanks that it's done. Take care of your affairs full on, no slouching—go to the gym, pay your bills early, things like that. Life doesn't reward shirking or laziness or malingering. Enjoy the rest of your life so much that you don't need it…whatever that *it* is you're waiting for. Live in gratitude and as love. Just create a life so wonderful that the dream—the relationship, the part, the whatever—is the rose on the icing of the cake. It's coming. Just enjoy now. That'll help it happen faster. And it won't matter if it does or not, because you're happy with life and yourself now. That's all that really matters."

"See? You're as wise as anything or anyone you quote."

I've always been absurdly impressionable. Movies, books, songs, even advertisements have the strangest impact on me. When I was thirty-seven I dragged my hapless boyfriend to Paris practically for the sole reason—I kid you not—of that line in "The Ballad of Lucy Jordan" by Marianne Faithfull. So he and I drove a sports car in Paris one warm day. I even wrote a screenplay about my rendition of Lucy—that's how much that song affected me. Back to Paris, that little drive was mildly entertaining. But it definitely satisfied something in there. And I didn't even have to go crazy like Lucy Jordan to feel my hair blowing in the warm wind.

Well, that crazy thing might be a little debatable.

I let it sit for a few days. Finally, the following Saturday I joined her on the deck, barely registering that her cocktail hour had moved up from five o'clock to three.

"No. You know what? I have a fascinating life and it involves movies and stories and understanding people and what motivates them. I don't have a I'm-ready-for-my-close-up-Mr.-DeMille moment, but Gloria does. She did that for me so I don't have to. I can go exploring other things. Renée wore that granny underwear in *Bridget Jones's Diary* so we could laugh at our own stuff and, well, maybe not ever wear that kind of underwear."

Cyn took another sip of wine.

"We laugh at ourselves, we laugh at the human condition. We're all wise. We all know things. I want to draw on everyone."

Maybe if I hadn't given such a gruff answer she wouldn't have killed herself.

As for that wisdom I spouted—where in the world did all that come from? Why in the world didn't I follow that? I toned my quoting way down around her, though, for what remained of her life.

But Cyn, much as I loved you then and love you still and always will, I love quoting movies. Some people quote philosophers. Many a movie is a current form of philosophy.

And on another day came this: oh, Cyn, I'm so sorry. I take it back. Not just that conversation—any conversation where it wasn't enough, where I wasn't enough to make you want to stay here.

If grief had a color, what would it be? Gray? Black? What about depression or loneliness? What color would they be? Maybe the same.

If joy had a color, what would it be? Coral? Watermelon? And how would someone turn the gray to coral? The black to watermelon?

Under normal circumstances (i.e. when I'm not wracked with guilt for killing my BFF), I love green. I love blue. I love pink and purple. I'm not crazy about brown or tan. I take gray days as a personal affront.

I caught a glimpse of myself in the mirror. When the hell did I buy this big, bulky gray sweatshirt? I thought Cyndi broke me of that habit years ago. I quickly took it off, replaced it with a streamlined pink one, and hopped in the car.

The Eagles sang about that hotel in this here state. Remember the last line of the chorus, the one about checking out but not leaving?

Oh, yes, you can. Have you met my friend?

Oh, Trish...maybe it's time for a new groove in your record.

Perhaps.

Notice I still said things that blur the lines? In a way. Kind of. I could still be very *ish*. Maybe I could be less *ish* and more definitive.

Maybe tomorrow. *Ish.*

It's the last three letters of my name, after all.

It seemed absolutely insane to go from trying to get a superhuman number of things done in a day to sometimes doing absolutely nothing.

It's okay to just sit, you know, I said to myself. Staring into space is actually a huge part of the creative process.

No, I didn't know that, I responded to myself. I always need to be moving forward. Sitting still feels like moving backward.

You do it at the beach, my self continued the conversation.

I know. That's different.

Those years and years of multitasking more than was even necessary, fitting just one more thing, and just one more after that, into my day, were all to, oh, I don't know, make me feel useful? Make me feel worthy?

Ever look around and see all the people looking at their phones at every stop light? I would do that, but I sink into things so quickly and all my attention goes to the article or post or whatever. Then I'd actually get irked when the light turned green. Lately I'm happy to avoid lots of little irkles all day long, especially when I'm getting a green light!

Ever notice how when you're in a super-big hurry, that's when you end up behind the super-slow lady at the supermarket? Or somewhere else—it doesn't have to be the supermarket. Maybe it's just better to not ever be in a hurry. I mean, I've done that with giving myself plenty of time to drive somewhere, but then I give myself a million things to do while I'm waiting for whatever appointment. The only way I could lighten up on myself was to give myself plenty of time *all* the time. It added facets to my life that I'd never had before. I was always chomping at the bit, trying to get the next thing done to check it off my list. Well, it could get checked off, but another one was just going to take its place momentarily. And I really don't enjoy the chomping-at-the-bit thing.

I don't want to get to the end of my life and find I rushed all the way through it trying to get the next thing done, the next thing checked off the to-do list, and realize

I didn't do things to live, I lived to do things. Things have to get done, of course. But the being is where life happens. Oh! Just look at all this stuff it takes to be a star. No one wants to watch a star doing all the doing that it takes; everyone just wants to see the star being all the being that all of the doing took to get there.

Yes, I'm babbling again. But many a truth is said in babble.

I was always in a hurry...like I had some fire-breathing temple dragon inside, rushing me along. To get to what? To relax? I could've relaxed the whole time. I could've been in peace and serenity instead of rushing rushing rushing to finish the next thing so I could...eventually...relax....which I rarely did.

Ever hear that story about the Mexican fisherman and the American businessman? I'm sure you have, but here it is again. The American went on vacation in Mexico and saw a fisherman playing his guitar in a restaurant. To make the longer story not so long, the businessman recommended the fisherman buy a fleet of fishing boats and grow a lucrative business, all so he could...relax and play his guitar in the restaurant at night.

Let enough be enough and happy be happy.

Cut to the Chase

Back at my place, the beach...the one with the dogs... and—

"Trish?"

Seriously? Frig—not him again.

"Loafin'?"

The simple question from the simple word made me smile. It was so.....real. So....right now. His shaggy friend tried to meld with my body again.

"Leia, no! Calm down!"

"Leia? As in Princess?"

"Guilty. Major *Star Wars* fanatic."

Jeff and Leia sat down with me, uninvited.

"Lucas almost didn't make that movie because there was so much negativity rolling all around it," he said. "So they say."

"Whoever they are."

"Look. Over there." He pointed to a couple walking along the beach with their dog. "They look very they."

I laughed. Something felt so good about the simplicity of the moment, with the ease of laughing. There was no pretense, nowhere else I had to be, nothing else needed right there, right then. That was so Wisconsin.

"They do," I smiled. "Look very they, that is."

He cut to the chase. "Would you like to have dinner sometime?"

"Sure." Awkward pause. "How about now?" I asked. "I'm kind of hungry."

He looked like someone just told him he won the lottery. Despite living inside this amazingly handsome and successful man that he'd become, I could tell the pipsqueak still talked—even reigned—inside his head. He should meet Fugly sometime.

Dinner was comprised of pasta and mostly him talking about his job because I suddenly turned into a mute.

"I never forgot that," he sighed, after telling me about exposing a family-values politician's mistress back when he was a young, hotshot reporter.

"But we do need to know that kind of thing."

"Right, we do. But it didn't have to come from me. I ruined two families. We need to expose hypocrisy, but it didn't have to come from me. There are plenty of reporters eager to do that. I'm not one of them."

"Maybe that's the best thing that happened to all of those people involved—the kids, too. They weren't living with lies anymore."

"Maybe." His expression told me he hadn't thought it of that way before. I watched a little bit of guilt ease out of his face.

"I prefer sports anyway, though," he said. "Must've been meant to be."

That wasn't something I'd expected a sports journalist to say, but there it was.

Jeff looked around for the waiter, who was nowhere to be found. He looked over at me, and I tried to hide that I'd been staring at him. "I heard ya lookin'."

I looked down, mostly so he couldn't see the tears in my eyes.

"Want to do this again sometime soon?"

No. "Yes."

I surrender. The title of this scene could be "Nice Guys Don't Finish Last; They Finish Best." Or, "Sweet Guy with Dog Meets Madwoman." Seriously.

Ribbit

I've kissed many, many frogs. Oh, that is so incredibly rude. What'd they think if they knew I considered them frogs? What would their mothers say? And what did they think of me?

Maybe they were hoping I'd turn into a Princess—or at least someone who knew she was a Princess. We're all royalty, really.

"I couldn't have said hi to your mom because I don't think I know her," I said because I couldn't think of a single other thing to say on our next...whatever it was. It wasn't a date—it felt too relaxed, chummier than that. We were at the dog beach at sunset again, where Leia was finally getting the idea that she could be with me without trying to be one with me.

"Yeah, you would. She's worked at the library for decades. Actually, my mom would flip out if I ever let her know we were hanging out," he replied.

We're "hanging out"? Well, maybe twice, not counting when we bumped into each other at Claude's house. Does that qualify as legitimate "hanging out"? Well, maybe that's what the whatever, this non-date-thing, was.

"She blames acting for my former wife's inability to commit. Actually, Wendy can commit just fine—for about six months at a time."

We were quiet for a bit.

"Tell me about your friend, the one who died."

"She was everything you'd think a human being would want to be: warm, funny, sunshiny, beautiful. She was— we were—I still am, I guess, in that endless yearning thing, yearning for more. Whatever is, isn't enough. I told her...." I stopped.

"What did you tell her?"

"Be grateful for what you have but expect more. It's what we do, as humans. We always want more. But gratitude is where more starts from."

"She had a very wise friend."

No, don't go there. Too late. "Then why did she kill herself?"

I sobbed and sobbed and sobbed as he held me in his arms. Again.

"Because I wanted to."

I looked up. He hadn't said it.

I'm really not crazy—I promise. I mentioned to you that I have voices in my head sometimes, but this was the first time that it wasn't any characters I was in the process of inventing—or me—who were talking.

So this second meltdown during our second "hanging out" should've definitely scared him away. Technically, the first meltdown was not during a hanging out.

"Want 2 go 2 beach again?" he texted a couple days later.

"Haven't I scared u off enuf?"

"Nah. I get grief. My dad died back in h.s., after u left. Better 2 cry than not."

So we "hung out" for a third time.

I walked into Cara's office.

"You met someone."

"Maybe," I smiled. As quickly as the smile came, though, it disappeared. Cara took me into her inner office and shut the door behind her.

"You don't have to die with her, you know."

"Huh?"

"I've lost lots of people," she said. "My parents died fairly young, my cousin who was my best friend died young of cancer, a favorite coworker committed suicide. It's hard to go on without them sometimes. Like, how dare we...keep living?"

The floor seemed to give way underneath me, and I sank into a nearby chair as the floodgates opened again.

"You were her bestest of best friends. But you don't have to follow her where she went."

Oh, the tears streamed.

"I didn't know...that's what...I was...doing."

"Of course you didn't." Cara let me cry for what seemed like hours.

"When's it going to get better?" I sobbed.

She wrapped her arms around me. "I don't know, honey. But I do know it will. It will. But you're here and alive. Please let just one person be in Cyndi's grave."

Any day could be the day that it gets better, that happily ever after begins.

CHAPTER 8

Thoughts While Waiting on My Oil Change....

I watched the people, just regular folks, around me. I've said that actors are such tender creatures, but we all are, really. I've said that it's amazing that society gets along as well as does, given the messed-up food, television, and pharmaceuticals we're served. It makes us lash out at each other sometimes—and it's amazing there's not more lashing out.

Wait, what was that? I heard you. Weren't you thinking something along the lines of hey, she auditions for roles on TV. That makes her part of that garbage. Well, I hope not. There are good shows and there's rot. There are even good commercials and there's rot. Didn't you love it when the Clydesdales helped bring that adorable puppy home to that equally adorable (and very hunky) guy? And how many issues does a show like *Grey's Anatomy*, for just one example, address? In addition to myriad illnesses, death, and grief, it covers domestic violence, gender dysphoria, drug addiction and recovery—the list could go on all day and night.

Back to these regular folks...they could just float about doing their thing. At the moment, their thing was keeping busy on their phones or laptops while they were waiting for the way-too-perky sweet young thing (give that woman a Valium!) to alert them that their car was ready. They weren't on their guard. They weren't looking down to keep from being recognized....or at least puzzled over with quizzical looks.

One time I saw a very famous—but who shall remain nameless—actor in a restaurant. Some elderly woman just plopped down next to her in the booth. The actor looked like she wanted to leap through the wall, and the other person with her was of no help whatsoever. The oldie proceeded to yak and yak like they were old chums. To her, they were—old chums, that is. We've all been watching this woman on the big screen for decades and decades. We've watched the lines form on her face. We recognize almost every nuance in her voice. We feel like we do know her.

It never crossed my mind—until it did—that if/when I "made it," that would probably happen to me, too. And I'd probably like it even less and freak out even more than that famous actor did.

But, speaking as one of those faces on the screen, people know us as our characters, not who we are. They feel a sense of familiarity with us and even an entitlement to us, since they've seen us so many times.

Ugh. Some guy was giving me the look. You know the one—the good old I-know-I've-seen-you-somewhere-and-I'm-going-to-stare-at-you-until-I-remember look. Hmm, the cell phone is the best of inventions for such times; I stopped looking around and stared at my phone. How did I not hear this text from Cara come in? I have a special alert for her, but I somehow missed it. She had another audition for me...yikes, with the fussiest casting director in town. She's not the only fussy one—just the fussiest. Casting directors can have no filters: "You're too thin/too fat/too old/too young/too beautiful/not beautiful enough."

Maybe that's why actor friends feel like they can say anything, too—because they hear it from the CDs so often. "You slouch too much." "You don't shine enough." "You gripe too much." "You don't think ahead enough." "You worry too much." Oh, mind your own struggle!

Actually, no one says anything to me about worrying anymore. (Wow.)

A photo of the dry-cleaning-store manager's sister stares out at me as I walk in. "Give to the Melanie fund," it says.

Apparently Melanie is dying. We're all dying really. And that's not necessarily a bad thing. And maybe the goal of this life isn't to live as long as possible, but as well as possible. We'd be insufferable if we lived forever.

After a few more errands, I drove home after dark—my favorite time to drive here, as you know, what with all the lights turning all the roads and buildings into the Magic Kingdom. The sappy songs were starting to annoy me (wow, now that's *sappy*), so I switched to classic rock. Bruce was singing about Mary dancing on her porch. In addition to being a great musician, he's such a poet, really. All songwriters are. Maybe we all are, when we're in our own particular groove. Heck, even the LA Lakers are poetry in motion (and this from a non-sports-oriented person).

"Thunder Road" ended and then Prince was singing about precipitation of a certain shade on the darker end of the rainbow spectrum (purple). Then David Bowie sang about being really great people, if just for this day. Oh, I want to cry when I hear David Bowie—I miss him so much. I once heard that he became a singer because he couldn't find someone to sing his songs the way he wanted them sung. Well, that's one way to get a dream going.

That song ended and then Tom Petty sang about the girl next door. What was this—the Dead Singers' Society coinciding with my-favorite-dead-musicians' hour? Well, except for Bruce, of course. I can't hear Tom's words without thinking of *Silence of the Lambs*. Oh, yeah. I sang and tapped on the steering wheel just like Brooke Smith did as Catherine Martin, right before she was abducted. Well, I'm sure just about everybody does that, right?

Speaking of Tom Petty, when he died a couple friends of mine shared some stories of how wonderful—and chatty—he was to them. He even remembered one from years before. "Hey, you're Marianne from the Macy's on Riverside in Sherman Oaks!" I haven't always been great with names, but I've tried to improve, with some success, after hearing that. It's just a nice touch to life.

The Red Carpet

There was suddenly this other nice touch to life...Jeff. What in the world was I going to do with this guy? He wasn't disappearing into the ethers like all the others. Of course, we hadn't had sex yet—that's usually what did it. Give it time.

But...this guy wasn't like most men I'd dated. He was sweet, kind, not looking for anything, content. Maybe he's an alien?

Nah, he just hailed from Wisconsin, where manners and contentedness were part of the schools' curricula. I must've missed that class on contentedness, though.

"How r u?" he texted.

"Living the dream," I texted back. "Want 2 go 2 a premiere?" Oh, that's just great, I thought. Now he's a public statement. What have I done?

It was a very small-time movie I'd played the lead in several years earlier. Sometimes movies, especially the smaller ones, take eons to finish. A child actor could be in middle school by the time the movie's done. Sometimes they don't even get done, for that matter.

I buy my special outfits in a small dress shop in Sherman Oaks, speaking of Marianne at the Macy's there. The owner, a master seamstress, alters everything that goes out the door so that it's a one-of-a-kind creation. This one was a sheath of turquoise, cocktail length, with a somewhat deep neckline and a jagged, lacey hem.

The red carpet—what a wild, wonderful experience that is. Thank goodness so many pictures are taken because if that one moment wasn't frozen in time that way, I'd forget it ever happened. It's really such a quick, blinding blur. After the first round of bulbs come more, plus calls to look this way or that. I can't see well for a few minutes after all those flashes.

We're all—every human—insecure to some extent. Actors are an especially insecure lot, but we're not allowed to show it so much. Who wants to see a slumped, bowed, insecure actor at the Academy Awards? No, we want to see polish and grace and ease and flow. So many years of training go into those one-minute walks and thirty-second interviews.

I was far from polish and grace and ease and flow, but each red-carpet walk got a little easier. "Just channel your inner Lady Gaga, honey," Cara once recommended.

After the blinding-flashbulb moments, Cara turned into a shepherd for her babe-in-the-woods. "Here, honey. Meet this person, meet that person. Oh, and have you met Mr. So-and-So and don't forget Ms. Such-and-Such."

In between our chats with industry folks, Cara chatted with Jeff. She flashed me a signal that she approved…a whole lot.

Then there came the old watching-myself-in-a-movie thing. I'd almost never been by myself in a scene as I wasn't usually a lead with all that air time, so I'd been spared that ECU (extreme close up) where I got to see all my pores—until that movie! OMG, it was hard. Was that really me? Seeing actors in real life can be startling, because the camera fills out people's faces so much. Seeing myself, even now……well, to me I look like a puffalump. Cara assures me time and again that I'm the only one seeing a puffalump up there.

If there's a panel after the movie, like there was with this one, that's a whole other ball of wax. I actually enjoy those, because I like to have the opportunity to sound intelligent answering questions and discussing the movie with the audience. Then there came that applause thing. At first it can be hard to stand there while people applaud. It took some practice for me to just stay and not want to dive into the footlights or disappear up into the rafters.

"Give them the gift of giving you something," Cara once coached. "They just received a gift from you and they want to give something back. Let them! Graciously receive their applause as that gift they want to give."

Of course, some of us humans, especially in LA, have no problem with applause. Lookatmelookatmelookatmeme-me-me-me-me-me-meeeeeeeeee! I-i-i-i-i-i-i-i-i-i-i-i-i-i! It's all about me-me-me-me-me-me. Okay, enough about me. What do you think of me?

I'm not that way. Well, maybe I am and I just don't know it.

Then there's the after-party in another mansion in the Hollywood Hills. Thankfully the dresses are so tight they're a constant reminder not to eat too much.

Something was slightly different this time. One of the producers stuck by me for a bit, and it wasn't in the usual Hollywood slimy way.

"Would you like to audition for a movie we're doing?"

With her ever-present radar, Cara was by my side in half a nanosecond, so she could talk business with him.

Jeff had never seen me in movie-star mode, even though the movie was pretty small beans. I wanted to tell that beaming gleam in his eyes to calm the frig down.

As the valet (hell, Chuck E. Cheese has valet parking in LA!) was getting Jeff's car, we wandered over to the side of the house and looked down on the vista of the Hollywood lights.

"I never grow tired of that," I whispered. "Ever hear the story of Jim Carrey and his five-million-dollar check?"

"Yes. He'd go up to look over the Hollywood lights and imagine himself being a great actor. He wrote himself a five-million-dollar check, right, and promised himself he'd cash it someday?"

"And the day he could cash it came much sooner than he expected."

We noticed the valet fellow was looking around for us, but it was hard to pull myself away from that view.

"It's like it's a lightscape, always reminding me what's possible."

He smiled.

As he drove me home, though, I tried to think of something to talk about that didn't involve a movie or this town. And what would I do with him when we got there? He picked me up at Cara's office, so he hadn't seen my (well, Cyndi's mom's) little hobbit house yet. I wonder what his place is like?

He didn't have much to say either, apparently. I mostly just gave him directions, and he made short comments about landmarks and neighborhoods here and there.

He parked in front of the house. So much for that awkward do-I-invite-him-in-or-not moment. He opened his door and quickly walked around the car to open mine. He helped me out of the car. (Even though it wasn't ball-gown length, the dress still wasn't easy to navigate in.)

He walked me to the front door and waited while I fished my key out of my clutch. Once I opened the door, he pecked me on the cheek, vamoosed back to his car, and disappeared into the night.

Uh, okay.

There's More to this Whole Crazy Thing Here

A few days later I returned to the spiritual center to work on my mailings to prisoners. I had a stack of letters waiting for me.

Get a load of this one from Texas: "I'm a tough, hardened criminal covered with tattoos," a man wrote. "But when I opened your letter, this wave of love rushed out and washed all over me. And I—this tough, hardened criminal—cried like a baby. Thank you."

A wave of love. This wasn't some woo-woo Northern California guy. There's so much more to this crazy thing called Life than we know.

Tears slipped down my face. For the first time in almost a year, they weren't tears of pain.

Jeff and I started doing more and more of the hanging-out thing. We'd mostly walk Leia on the beach or hike in the hills because both of us needed lots of nature time after our hectic workdays. I invited him to a couple of improv performances, and he sat in the front row and laughed the loudest. We went to the symphony one night and to a museum on a Sunday afternoon and to several premieres of friends' movies. We'd eat lunch or dinner after whatever event. If he'd picked me up, instead of us meeting somewhere, he'd still walk me to the door, peck, and vamoose.

That was fine with me. For the first time in my life, I didn't just want to tumble into bed with someone. Maybe it was growing older. Maybe it was growing up. Maybe it was....I don't know. Maybe it just was.

One thing about him that drove me bonkers was he Googled everything. I mean, *everything.* I'd mention a movie or an actor, and if he wasn't familiar with whatever or whoever, he'd Google whatever or whoever. One time we were watching a music video playing in a restaurant and he started Googling. He should've had a supply of T-shirts to wear every day that proclaimed LMGTFY (let me Google that for you).

"I hope you own stock in Google," I said once.

"As a matter of fact, I do," he replied.

"Can't you just watch the video?"

He looked at me in shock.

"I don't mean to be rude, but you're always Googling. Like—always."

"I want to know everything about them," he said, pointing to the musicians. "What makes them tick, why they wrote those songs, what the meanings of the lyrics are. Just let me."

Yikes—our first fight?

Well, I let him...for a while. "You are addicted to your phone!" I yelled the next week.

Actually, so am I and so is just about everyone else I know. Every now and again Cyn or I would shriek, "Where's my phone?" in ersatz distress. "It's not in my hand!"

Maybe it wasn't so fake, but we'd laugh.

"It's over there, it's over there!" one or the other of us would reassure the other.

"Phew!"

"Catastrophe narrowly averted once again!"

But he was something else altogether. Sure, he had to keep up with current events and do extensive research for his job. But still—his hand was never empty.

"Beats living in a library," he retorted.

But the next time we went out, I noticed his phone did not make it's every-other-minute appearance.

He got me back, though. I had a habit of grumbling at other drivers on the road.

"That hate you're spewing out to the driver is not only going to him or her—it's going back to you. And me, because I'm with you."

My spewing abruptly stopped.

The anniversary of Cyndi's death and her birthday, the next day, came and went. I totally chickened out. I kept myself super busy with clients. I also didn't drink anywhere near as much coffee as usual so I was asleep by eight o'clock both nights.

But she was back to being the first thing on my mind as I woke up. I was so tired of missing her. I tried making myself even busier; one way was by signing up for another round of acting classes, but my teachers started giving me the boot.

"Trish," my acting coach said, "just get out there and do it. I can't teach you anymore. I mean, I can—there's always more to learn, of course. But you have to do it. You just have to get out there and do it."

So I signed up for a workshop at my spiritual center. The main thing I remember the teacher saying was, "You don't need anyone else's approval! Do you approve of this yourself? If so, then there you have it. If not, change it. Your life is your creation. What do you want? Make it so."

I'm all over that, I thought.

And, fine, I'll tell you that I check in with a psychic/astrologer once a year. I like to cover all bases. I basically always ask the same thing: when am I going to make it? That year she didn't tell me about my North Node or where my Saturn was or anything like that—not that I ever really understood it all anyway. No, here's what she said this particular year: "You're the captain of your spaceship. You decide what you want and go make it happen."

"Skye, how are you always so happy and peaceful?"

"It's a choice," she smiled.

Frig. I knew that. I just never made that choice—not truly, anyway.

One time Cyn asked, "What do you think the chances of us getting what we truly want truly are?"

"Oh, I think there's a possible probability. Perhaps. Maybe."

"You know what the chances of making it in this town are?" she sighed.

"A hundred percent for the people who make it. It's the same as the lottery—the chances are slim to almost none, but they were a hundred percent for the person who won the Powerball Saturday night."

She wasn't having it. "What if we spend our whole lives yearning for this and never make it? I've spent my entire life yearning—yearning to grow up, yearning to find a boyfriend, yearning to get rid of the boyfriend, yearning for a better boyfriend, yearning for a better job, yearning to be a world-renowned actor."

"Maybe the idea is to be happy wherever we are, right where we are. Then it doesn't matter. Then it comes in."

Shit. I said that. I fucking said that. (Remember when I said I don't swear much, unless it's really something? This is really something.) We know this stuff. We *do*. But we forget it as quickly as we remember it.

Siri and I were having words again. We do that from time to time. I liked this new version of Siri better, though. The old one was churlish and schoolmarmish. But the new one could still sound snippy.

"I don't KNOW if that's a Starbucks I want! That's what I'm asking you for, you fucking bitch!" Okay, that was a slight overreaction, to be sure. She was only trying to help. About that lack of swearing thing, it's gone out the window lately.

But that day, even after canceling a few texts through her, she never lost her patience (AI is good that way). She just said, "Okay, Trish. Let me know if there's anything I can do for you."

I burst into tears at that. Yes, Siri, can you get me my knight in shining armor? My name in lights? A million bucks? My house by the ocean? My best friend back?

Could you take me away from all of this? Could you take the pain out of my heart?

One night in a restaurant (Spago, if you please), Jeff and I had a fight. I actually picked it with him, but it was after he picked on me for not knowing a current event—a rather obscure current event, I might add.

"Well we can't all be as perfect as you are," I hissed.

He didn't say anything, but his mouth did that thing his mouth would do when he wasn't exactly being forthcoming.

As my friends would quit the acting thing and move away, I suddenly had friends all over the place—San Francisco, Taos, Boulder, even Fayetteville, Arkansas. I met a guy from Kansas once who told me that feisty Kansans pronounce one of the rivers that runs through their beloved state the Ar-KAN-sas River, to keep the respect in the name.

I needed a good…something. Colorado sounded like a good something. So off I went to visit my friend there. The Denver airport smells like the tent we camped in when I was a kid; the top of the terminal—designed to look like the mountain peaks to the west as well as teepees that were on the Great Plains to the east—is made of something that smells very much like canvas, like a tent. There's also a blue bronco statue, with a diabolical-looking red eye, which killed its sculptor by falling on him. That's so not nice—to kill one's creator like that. I think that eye had something to do with it.

The strangest thing about Denver is that the streets are empty by nine PM because everyone wakes up at five to go climb a mountain, jump on their bikes, or run a marathon. When I got back to LA and was driving home from the airport at midnight, it was a shock to see so many cars on the road. What in the world are all these people doing up so late, I thought. We humans certainly can adjust fairly quickly to new surroundings, and then it takes a day or two to snap back.

My friend Gwen, who was Colorado pretty before she even moved here, lived in Boulder. She wanted to take me to see a psychic medium who talks to dead people.

"I think it'll be good for you," Gwen urged. "Maybe Cyndi will say something."

I'd wanted to leave LA to get away from Cyndi (and Jeff) for a weekend. But I agreed to go, intrigued at the possibilities.

I saw a book once where the title was something like *Can Ghosts Watch You Shower?* Ewwwww! The thought gave me chills. The older you get, the more people in your life die, so the more crowded it'd be in there. Actually I doubt they'd be all that interested.

Other than that batty book title, I didn't think about ghosts very often, and I definitely didn't have a whole lot of experience communicating with the afterlife. Maybe Cyndi did speak to me that time on the beach and that other time in her bedroom when the curtain moved, but I attributed both of those events more to my very overactive imagination. Yeah, yeah—that's what it was.

Gwen and I sat through a bunch of dead folks wanting to talk to an aunt, a daughter, a spouse. There was even one ghost who was pestering the medium.

"There's a young woman, about nineteen or so," the medium said.

A number of people stood up, scattered around the large auditorium.

"She committed suicide," the medium continued, "and she wants to talk to her parents."

All of the people standing sat down except for a man and woman near the back. They held each other tightly.

The medium addressed her comments to the couple. "She wants to say that she loves you and that there was nothing you could've done. Not a single thing."

The couple burst into tears. I'm sure everyone present had tears in their eyes. Their relief was palpable, even in that large room.

Gwen took me to a small kirtan in Boulder the next night...and that's where the young woman's words hit me. As the lovely older woman in the front of the room sang and played her harmonium, and the audience members chanted with her or responded to her calls, I dissolved into a puddle of tears. They wouldn't stop. My friend put her arm around me, and my tears flowed and flowed.

These were different tears, though...not of loss as much as relief. "There was nothing you could have done," the young woman had said through the medium. "Not a single thing."

Maybe I should go to more kirtans, I thought, once I returned to LA. I did, and they were fun, but I didn't experience another breakdown and breakthrough like that one.

The radio was sending me a message again. Thank you, R.E.M. I've heard that "losing my religion" can be a way of saying you're at the end of your rope. Tie a knot—hang on tight!

Or maybe let go.

Speaking of hanging, hanging out with Jeff (which we were apparently still doing despite my rudeness at Spago and running away to the Rockies for a weekend) was a whole new experience for me. Now that he'd stopped his Googling habit, at least while in my company, he was the only person I knew who wasn't looking for anything. Well, Skye definitely oozes contentment, and Cara seems pretty happy with her lot. Okay, he was the only person in the near vicinity of my age who was cowlike (meaning...content). Maybe it's the Wisconsinite in him. Why didn't I catch some of that?

Oh, but he pissed me off sometimes. How can anyone be *so* easygoing and content?

One night over sushi at Sugarfish, I was in rambling mode. If this didn't scare him off, nothing would. "It's like life is a friggin' jigsaw puzzle, and I don't even know what the picture looks like, but here I am putting pieces together, and as I put them together the picture shows up! What's up with that? Why don't I have the picture beforehand?"

"Maybe you do. You just don't know it."

I hate it even more when he's brilliant.

Meanwhile, at Some Point During the American Revolution

I found myself on the set of a movie taking place during the American Revolution. The guy playing the young General Washington was quite hot. Whoever thought of George Washington as young and hot? Well, maybe Martha did back in the day. I still feel twenty-five, but I'm not, and I don't want to be construed as anything close to cougarlike, so I kept my distance even when he mildly flirted with me.

I went to my car at lunchtime to take a nap. (No, there wasn't a trailer for this crowd member who had just a few lines.)

Ever notice how when you're drifting off to sleep, the truth slips in because the usual guards are down? Jeff's as hot and handsome as this "George" is, I thought as I drifted. And beyond that, Jeff has substance...intelligence...depth...age appropriateness...all the things I'd want in a mate.

"And he's available. That's his problem."

Who in creation said that? That was from the truth part, unchecked by the half-snoozing guards.

Forget sleeping. I was wide awake with tears running down my cheeks. Frig, I'll have to go get my makeup touched up.

Much as my mind didn't want to acknowledge it, realization had struck. If Jeff was available, he could...he could....he could *die*. Like Cyn, like Brian.

I could take Brian dying. It wasn't fair, but that's how it goes sometimes—someone's sick and he or she doesn't live all that long. I understood that; it's logical even if it's unlikeable; it's an unpleasant part of life. His death might've been a dark cloud over my life for years, maybe even decades, but it made sense.

Cyndi dying....I just didn't understand. It wasn't logical. It made no sense at all. It sucked.

And she wasn't even a mate. I don't know how I could live through a death of someone even closer to me.

This movie was on a studio set...one of the fancy studios with the pearly (okay, maybe not, but close) gates. Friggin' Hollywood. Most of us have a love/hate relationship with it. I'd been realizing that Cyn must've suffered with depression, but in a land of perfect weather and perfect people, with a focus on wealth and power, not the underbelly of human emotions, we don't really talk about it here. I was starting to understand.

I was also starting to understand why successful people kill themselves here, in part thanks to the reactions of the fanboys on the set once again treating me like I'm someone special. (No fangirls—the script and continuity women often act as if they're doing us all a favor by being there.) Most of us—maybe 99.99999999 percent of us—are born with some form of low self-worth. If that hasn't been healed, at least somewhat, by the time someone becomes a star, the constant adulation could drive someone insane. There's such a disconnect between how the world is treating them and how they feel inside. I also understand why musicians tend to take so many drugs. We all have access to the music of the spheres, the creative muse, but it can be scary. It's so big. We're so big. But we've forgotten. Drugs tone down the distance between who we might think we are (small) and who we really are (big).

I got back to the set and wasn't exactly polite to people. Blech. Way to get more roles, Trish—be a bitch to the AD.

If I was a nasty she-beast in that moment, what else could I have been? Yes, I hear you—*not* a nasty she-beast. But that's what I was in that moment. Given all the factors, that's what I was. In another moment, with another set of factors, I wouldn't have been in nasty she-beast mode. So it's the factors……

Put another way, as I said to myself as I drove home later that night, I am doing the fucking best I can. I can do better, and I will. But what I've done is the best I could do at the time with what I had and have. So just shut the fuck up. Perhaps what I have is even enough.

Then came something I wasn't expecting. "Fuck you, Cyn," I erupted to the dashboard. "Fine, I surrender. I will cry about you every single day for the rest of my whole fucking life. I'll always regret that I didn't say enough, that I said too much, that I didn't see it coming, that I should've known. It was all my fault. Your entire fucking, beautiful, gold-ticket life was in my hands and I blew it."

I suddenly found myself parked on the side of the road screaming at the top of my lungs. "You had so much— you were so funny, so hip, so gorgeous, so happening, so delectable, so delightful. You were such a bright light. You were so amazing."

"So are you."

Imagined or not...the answer was real. Whether it came from her or from me imagining...it was from her. It was from me. Same thing.

Someone—a someone who can "see" and "hear" things not necessarily of this world—once told me that we can ask for signs. I remember doing that long before I met that person. Back in Wisconsin, before Fugly had faded, I once queried the nighttime sky, "What in the world am I going to be or do with this life?" A star shot across the western sky. The interpretation of that could have been so many things. What happened, in and of itself, wasn't the answer...the answer could be whatever I interpreted from what happened. I took it literally and went west to be a star.

That "seer" also told me we can ask questions and hear answers—maybe not from a particular person or directly from the heart of the Universe, but in the same way we can get signs...which is coming from the heart of the Universe, I guess.

"Cyn," I said to the air in the car, "if you were here, what would you say to me?" Nothing. Silence.

I started the car and on came the radio. Glenn Frey was singing the last line of "Desperado." I can't quote the lyric, as you know, so let me go a little Yoda on you again: Let someone love me, I should, before too late, it is. (Got it now?)

I burst into tears again. I think I've cried more in the fourteen months since Cyn died than I did in my whole life beforehand. And for months right after her death I couldn't cry at all. The other times certainly made up for those earlier days.

What if it was already too late?

It wasn't.

Back at the Front Door, Take Twenty. And.... Action!

The pecking and vamoosing was still happening. I was getting way over my initial hesitation about just tumbling into bed. Was he trying to drive me bananas?

On the walkway to the front door one night, I stopped. "Would you like to come in?"

"I thought you'd never ask."

"What? You've always taken off like a bat out of hell!"

He laughed but didn't say anything until we were inside and he texted a neighbor to take care of Leia. (I didn't even think about the presumption in that at the time.) "Wow. What a beautiful home."

He followed me into the kitchen where I poured us a couple glasses of Chardonnay.

"I think I'm getting ready to find something new," I sighed.

"Is that an advertisement?" he chuckled.

I was aghast. "I....uh.....no!"

Wine? What wine? His lips were on mine, and that was all she wrote.

So *this* is what making love is supposed to be like— actually making *love*? Not just going through the motions that the human animal has been doing for millennia. I'd been missing the love part, even those few times I thought I was in love. Oh, sure, it was fun (usually), but it wasn't this. I wasn't expecting a.....heart-opening, heart-awakening thang. And, no, this wasn't because I'd been out of service (or servicing) for more than a year.

Hands and a tongue here and there before was nice. They brought sparks, but not this—not electricity flooding me and lighting up the room, the block, the galaxy.

It was slow, too—another thing I wasn't used to. With all those quick one-night-stands or weekend flings or even the odd boyfriend, it was always done in an urgent, rushed, flurry, which I'd mistaken for passion. That was rutting. This wasn't.

The other people I'd stumbled into bed with were... impatient Type-A personalities. Jeff was like comfy blue jeans and Sunday mornings (the scrumdiddlyumptious kind). There was no rushing—we had forever.

"Whaaaaat?" My first thought the next morning was not quite as comfortable. "Whose arms are around me?" I was about to scream until I remembered. Jeff. Oh, no. JeffJeffJeff. OMG, what have I done? I was so used to greeting my days alone and with a sore heart. Actually, it was almost noon because we were up until four. Well, *that* was a nice night to remember, come to think of it. Yum.

I really had to pee. But I had nothing on, and suddenly the distance from the bed to the bathroom seemed like it was a mile. He saw me last night, but showing my altogether in full daylight is altogether a different thing.

This never really bothered me before. I never really cared all that much before. Plus, I've had very little clothing on in some movies, but even that didn't prepare me for this audience of one.

Fine. Just fine. I crawled out of bed and disappeared into the bathroom, Olympic-sprinter style. A glance in the bathroom mirror told me that at least I was crushing the JLL—the just-laid-look hair. And for very good reason!

When I came back out, Jeff was sitting up in bed waiting for me, watching.

"You are not forty-one," he smiled. "And there's nothing but amazing underneath all that amazing."

I laughed and crawled back into bed with him.

"You have the most beautiful body, Trish," he said. "It matches your heart."

Oh, but you don't hear how much my heart kvetches. Actually, the heart would never kvetch. Scratch that.

"Even my skinny white-girl's butt?" I joked because I couldn't think of anything else to say.

"It's perfect," he smiled. "Just like the rest of you." And the way he said it, I knew he wasn't just saying it. Maybe I'll keep this one.

As for him, he'd outgrown his pipsqueak, geeky body in more ways than one. But he was a gentle giant, a playful, cuddly bear.

Hours later, still in bed, I said, "You're so tender."

"Ruff!" he barked. Then, "Grrrrrrrrrrrrr."

I laughed…and laughed…laughed…. Could it all have been this easy all along, if only I'd let it?

"Are you crying?" he asked.

"A little."

"Why?"

"Just…..happy."

He twisted some strands of my wild curls (no flatiron yet that day) around his finger.

"Just saying."

"Just hearing. Me, too."

Oh, it felt so incredibly, amazingly wonderful to cry tears of joy again.

I made him Ketogenic pancakes (Google a recipe—they're delish) for breakfast, which we had at five PM. As we ate, a flicker of fear passed through me.

Jeff must've seen it in my eyes because he took my hand and said, "We got this."

CHAPTER 9

The Lines on My Face

If I ever sing in public, I sound kind of like Brandi Carlile. There are high parts, low parts, screechy parts—but the kind of screechy that put goosebumps on your blood. That's kind of the story of my life.

Dad taught me enough guitar chords for me to look like I know what I'm doing when the film includes a hippie party, a church youth group (back when), or a girl band. They put other music over it, of course. I can't remember if he taught me much of anything else. Mom taught me to drive....now *there* was a harrowing experience.

Dad.

"Your father died."

No. I can't go through this again, I thought as I clicked off the phone with Mom. But my father dying was a completely different animal. He was much older, for one thing—almost eighty. For another, I hadn't lived with him in many years. Plus, there's a logic to a parent dying, not to a dear friend disappearing out of the blue into the blue.

But, like Cyn, there was no preparation. He just keeled over at his workbench in the garage from an aneurism. Can't anyone stick around to say goodbye? From what I hear from friends, though, that's worse. Plus, we can always say good-bye, whenever. They can hear us—I'm convinced of that now.

You should care more, I said to myself as I stared out the plane window on the flight back. I tried to care more than I did. The man was my father, after all. I was sad, but not that he'd died—I was sad that he'd cloaked his life. It wasn't a real, full life; it wasn't even a possibility because he didn't entertain possibilities. It wasn't even a dress rehearsal. It would've been one thing if he'd been happy with his lot in life, but he wasn't.

I said as much to Jeff as I drove to my little town from the airport.

"Trish, your father came here to evolve his soul. He didn't really have to *do* anything."

He drove me stark raving mad sometimes. Especially when he was right. Who was this guy? Where did he come from?

Right—I know…he comes from my hometown. I meant bigger than that.

Maybe Dad was just fine living life at his workbench, where he could take things apart and put them back together better than they were before. Who am I to judge? But I took one long (nineteen-years-long) look at him doing that and swore I'd see my dreams come true.

Back to Brandi's song, which suddenly popped up on the radio several times….Here I lived in the land of plastic surgeons. If we erase all those lines, how will anyone know who we are and where we've been?

Skye has plenty of lines, but she looks natural, comfortable, not perpetually surprised or like she has platypus lips. She once said that facelifts could be avoided altogether if we'd all just keep reminding each other how beautiful we truly are.

I'd only been back the once, the time of the craft fair, since Cyn died. I expected to find Mom deep in her cups. She wasn't.

"I was going to tell you," she said. "I went into rehab."

I didn't say anything since shock had taken hold of every cell in my body. Her face hadn't looked this clear and vibrant since before Brian's final descent—and her husband just died!

"Wha-wha-what happened?"

"Cyndi died."

"Uh, yeah. I'm kind of aware of that."

"And I saw her parents at her memorial. They were inconsolable. Part of me realized that I hadn't been there for you for so long. I could've lost another child and never really even known who you were."

I couldn't talk.

"I went into rehab before you came back the last time, but I didn't stay with it. I went again right after you left, and by the grace of God, one day at a time, I'm doing it."

I didn't even care that she was speaking in program jargon and about God. This was...well, Cyn's death was less of a surprise than this. That's some surprise!

"When were you going to tell me?"

"I wanted to make sure I had something to tell you first."

I traced a design on the tablecloth, trying to avoid her gaze. The house was cleaner than I'd ever seen it.

"Honey, I'm so sorry. All those years...."

"Honestly it was what it was," I started to babble. "It just was. What it was, I mean. I didn't know anything different. It made me want to go off and be something wonderful.

"You can be something wonderful in your own hometown, you know."

"Uh, that's okay. Thanks, anyway."

We laughed until we cried.

I hadn't seen my brother during my last few trips home, and his life had taken a big switch, too. Kevin worked in the same factory as Dad, and was following in his footsteps another way (as was I)—not doing the marriage-and-family thing until later in life. And none too soon! His fiancée, about ten years younger, yet another similarity to Mom and Dad, was about six months pregnant.

"We're planning a September wedding," she told me.

I wasn't sure if she was timing it to have the baby still inside her or in her arms, but I smiled like a good future sister-in-law. And I'd have a niece soon! I didn't tell them this, but that little girl was going to be completely spoiled rotten by her aunt.

Another similarity—my soon-to-be-sister-in-law was a secretary, like Mom had been. (I don't think I ever told you what she did…sorry!)

"You doing okay?" Kevin asked me. That's big for him—over the years his face has been glued to comics, then to video games, and then to his phone.

"Yeah. You?" Another great conversationalist here.

"Yeah."

"I'm happy for you, Kev."

"Same here for you, Trish."

Not the deepest of conversations, you might think. But it was for us—we'd never said anything like those words to each other before.

Jeff flew out just for the funeral and then back the next day, as he was on assignment and I was going to linger.

Oh, that's his mom, I thought as he arrived with the town's favorite librarian at the funeral. Did he tell me that? Probably. It's been quite a year. I remembered her well—the short, plump, happy woman who loved her books and loved helping lonely adolescents find wisdom and perhaps better worlds in those shelves.

Jeff sat with me, though, and I saw lots and lots of smiles. There are few stories better than *The Ugly Duckling,* and even rarer are the two ugly ducklings from the same small town finding each other years and miles away.

I had a dream about Cyn the night of my father's funeral.

"What makes you think you could've saved me?" she demanded. "And who says I needed saving? What garage do you park your ego in, anyway?"

Keep Coming Back

I sat next to an older man on the flight home. "Older" always seems to be twenty years older than wherever we happen to find ourselves in the moment, but he was far older than that.

In addition to driving, flying is a place I do my deepest thinking. My mind went into reverie mode as I stared out the window. Middle-aged…that's technically what I am now, I thought, although I certainly don't feel it. Well, maybe I do at times. And those lines cropping up announce it.

I'd watched this old man trying to get into his seat on the plane, obviously in pain, and I had infinite compassion for him. With every passing day, that possibility comes closer and closer; it's not as far ahead of me as it once was. I flashed back on a young twenty-something I'd seen recently, shaking her head, rolling her eyes, believing she holds all the wisdom in the world. And I had infinite compassion. That possibility (and reality) is not too far behind me.

Jeff picked me up at the airport. We didn't talk much, but he held my hand as he drove me to my house...to Cyn's house, that is. It was starting to slip away from my heart. I looked at the Hollywood sign off in the distance and my palm trees lining the street.

Oh, Hollywood. You're so...fascinating. You're so...ridiculously rough on these oh-so fragile creatures known as humans. You're so...beautiful (in some places). You're so...ugly (in other places). You're so...Hollywood.

"The industry" can chew us up and spit us out like we're a nasty-tasting piece of garbage. So why would I do it? It's not the red-carpet moments, per se, although they're certainly fun. But they're also few and far between. Sitting on set for hours to sink into character for five minutes of filming isn't everyone's idea of a day well spent.

In various and sundry dressing rooms for my odd modeling and acting gigs, I noticed that women with straight hair would plug in their curling irons while women with curly and wavy hair would plug in their flat-irons. Women with freckles (including me) would use tons of makeup to cover them up; other women would add beauty marks. Some white women would try to look more ethnic; some ethnic women would try to look less so. Sometimes it made me want to go full-out crazy.

I know why I do it...because Dorothy's journey home is everyone's journey. Because Frodo's mission lives in each one of us. Because the big tales are the tales of the bigness in each one of us. Because the portrayals of pettiness in one of us are the portrayals of the pettiness that lives in us all. Because magic happens when the lights dim and the screen lights up. In fact, a screenwriting teacher once said that we do this screenwriting thing because when we were little kids, we'd go to the theater, the lights would dim, the music would swell, the screen would light up, and...we fell in love.

Movies are make believe, yes. But they're an art form relaying magic and new ideas for new worlds, even if they look just like the world we live in. We are captivated by unusual camera angles and lighting. Music sends chills down our spines. The traveling troubadours of old did that, but not on such a big scale. They were once the main storytellers. Now there are so many stories being told—on the big screen, on the little screen, in books, in songs, in art, in every social-media post.

I do this because movies have cracked open my heart and left it bigger than it was before, unable to go back to the smaller size it once was. I do this because there's nothing on Earth I'd rather do.

We can read a news story, like the one about the gang rape of Cheryl Araujo in New Bedford, Massachusetts, in 1983, and understand it—some. But watching Jodie Foster get attacked by one man after another on a pool table gives us sight, sound, texture, context, and horror. We can hear about the sex trade around the world, but seeing the girls enslaved in *Trafficked* gives us another viewpoint. We sell emotion and feelings, so audiences can experience them without necessarily having to live through them. But we open them up to have empathy for those who do have to live through such things.

In so many ways the world seems to be growing and evolving into a better version of itself. And in so many ways it seems to be doing the exact opposite. But with the Trumps and Harvey Weinsteins and other little-boy kings disintegrating and falling from power right in front of us, we do see a chance for true mightiness to rise. The thing about people like that is they render themselves no longer relevant, with the help of more and more people saying, "Enough!"

People think of Hollywood as a froufrou, light-weight industry. It's not. It can literally move mountains and change policy and draw attention to important issues.

It's also the other things people disdain it for, too, to be sure. There's the odd Humvee taking up two compact spaces. It's a land of borrowed glory and reflected fame— like that roadie I dated who tried to snitch his coolness from the superstar he worked for. It has massive amounts of drugs, pyramid schemes, and orgies—but hey, lots of places have those. It also has some of the most mystical people, talented people, compassionate people—often all combined into one with the druggies and crazies.

It's part comedy, part drama. Part spiritual existential reach, part uneventful downtime. Part tragedy, part ecstasy. Part shrinking, part growth experience. Even comedy isn't as banal as it might seem. I've often talked about actors (and all of us) having to dive deep; comedians definitely have to do that to let us laugh at ourselves. What a gift—to enable folks to chuckle as we showcase the human condition and allow us all to further understand the complexities of living in this body on this planet at this time.

We all travel a hero's journey. Even my dad at his workbench. Cyn, too, wherever she is now.

I didn't mean for this to turn into a *Mr. Holland's Opus*, but that's exactly what it is. We all have something special. We all bring something to the table. If we weren't here, the table would be missing a very important guest, and the world would be missing a vital gift that only we can bring.

One of those thousands of memes floating around lately has two rabbits with carrots. One rabbit's carrot has beautiful, amazing, bushy greenery—but just a measly little carrot under the ground. Meanwhile, the other rabbit's beautiful, lush, meaty (I suppose I should say veg-y, but you get the idea) carrot is mostly underground with just a wisp of greenery. So much of the world is judged by what we can see; the most important part is what we can't. Perhaps no place on Earth is that truer than here.

I went to my place, the beach in Malibu. What if I've done every single thing in my whole life wrong? I haven't, of course, but what if I did? So what?

What if it's okay right now, just as it is? I said to myself, Self (just kidding), stop grumbling about what life has done to you. It almost doesn't matter what life has done to you. What matters is what you're doing to life.

I surrender. It's all fine. I'm fine. Maybe what I have is just fine. Nobody wants to hear about a middle-to-middle story anyway. Everyone wants the rags-to-riches story. The born-in-a-log-cabin to the mansion-in-Malibu story. No one wants to hear about a middle-class existential crisis. But sometimes that's what it is, perhaps.

I sat and let the feeling of peace just come over me. It was like I was an overstuffed air mattress and a tiny hole was letting air seep out. Every inch of me just relaxed into the sand.

It could've been this easy all along, just like Jeff—but I had this thing come my way...and I had that thing come my way...then there was this thing...and....

I surrendered. Completely.

As I drove home, it occurred to me that most of my misery was of my own making. Sometimes the penance for the imagined sins is worse than for the real ones.

Perhaps if I just let myself feel sad when Brian died, I might've not had to turn to rampant worry. It's not a great way to live, that's for sure.

Plus, now that I know how grief works, at least as an adult and not a child in shock and denial, I'll probably pull over to the side of the road and scream some more here and there. And that's just fine.

After Ever Happily

The next week I got a great role in a great movie. It wasn't the lead role, but it was a great one. I haven't written the speech for accepting the Oscar for Best Supporting Actress, but I might.

The movie isn't with a big studio, but the director is a real up-and-comer I'd worked with before. I pitched her one of my screenplay ideas, and...she's interested. Not the LA kind of interested, have your people meet my people kind of thing, either—the real kind. I think this is the beginning of a beautiful friendship.

Funny how when the feelings have their way, life can have its way again. Remember Glenn Close's character in *Fatal Attraction*? She told Dan (Michael Douglas's character) that she was not going to be ig*nored*. Feelings can be like that, knife and all. Inviting them out for an afternoon to feel them, deal with them, and let them go doesn't mean they'll stay through the passing of the next season. It's more likely they will stay through the passing of the next season if they're not felt, not dealt with. Grief, surrender...all they want is to be felt. But on their time.

I also shook off all the shoulda-coulda-wouldas. Now *that* was a job. I think I had some help. (Thanks, Cyn.)

As of now, unlike in *Lala Land*, I haven't made it big—I've made it medium. But, also unlike *Lala Land*, I did get the guy. Jeff asked me to marry him. Yeah, it's a little fast, but he's the one. And I should know, given how many fellas in the town have been lucky enough to call me their date. (I'm trying that kind of thinking on—can you tell? Maybe it doesn't quite fit yet but it's getting there.) There's always been a madness to my method, and it finally seems to be working.

I called Cyndi's mom to tell her I was finally ready to move. There was a for-sale sign in the yard the next day. She was so patient with me, but once I was ready, I guess she figured there was no time to waste. I moved in to

Jeff's house in Topanga Canyon, and we started looking for a place that could be ours.

The other thing about "getting there" is by the time we get there, we've already become the person we needed to be to get there, so it's not as big a deal. It feels normal and less miraculous. Okay—maybe it feels a little miraculous.

And what happened after I kind of made it and married Jeff? I wanted something else. That's our nature. That's who we are. We don't just sit there. We make things. We create things. Maybe wanting an Oscar gets replaced with growing a garden. (Possible probability time flash— I actually do win an Oscar, once I turned my attention to growing a garden! It all works out when it doesn't have to.)

You know what? I spent almost my entire life wanting to be other people when in reality I had a pretty good deal going—if I would've just let it be good. I had so many people on a pedestal. Cue, for example and as I mentioned, Uma Thurman and Quentin Tarantino. *Pulp Fiction* and then *Kill Bill* were movements, and they were superstars. Behind the curtains, though, as we now know, things certainly weren't as they appeared. Okay, I'm changing the point here, mid-paragraph. Truth be told, that pedestal should be even higher but for a very different reason. I *truly, truly* admire Uma now—even more than I did before...along with Ashley...and Rose...and Salma...and Angelina...and Cara...and Gwyneth...and Lucia...and all the courageous women (and men, too) from all walks of life all over this planet.

Cue Cyn in this new point, as well—she really looked like she had it all. Cue almost anyone, really. We don't know what people have had to deal with, and we just can't compare ourselves to them. Practically every one of us deserves to be on a pedestal.

Remember back in the beginning when I talked about my screenwriting professor telling us that we can't have a story called *The Valley of the Happy People*? That a story needs conflict to show contrast, along with character development to show transformation? In other words, as I said, stories are just like this life we have here. Well, hopefully....hopefully we come out transformed, unless we die first. But then the transformation takes place on some other journey in some other place and time. Maybe we come back here; maybe not. But matter can never be destroyed, only transformed. That's us—we can't truly be destroyed....only transformed.....no matter what path we take. Ultimately, we can't get it wrong.....we can for a while, but our ship will right itself. Well, on the other hand, it might just sink, and that's fine, too. (Oh, Cyn.)

The highways around here are a metaphor for life. It never fails—as soon as I let someone in front of me, graciously, someone does the same for me. It's no coincidence; it's happened too many times. You let someone in front of you (anywhere), and then someone else will let you in front of them. What in the world is so hard to understand about that? It's not even doing to others as you would have done unto you because if you don't really care about yourself, you wouldn't really want people to treat you well. Witness all those abusive relationships. So you could ask, "How would I treat the person I regard as the most precious in my life?" Then treat everybody like that and see it come back to you. Unfortunately, too often we don't see the most precious person in our lives as ourselves, but we should.

Sunday morning I woke up in Jeff's arms. Oh, Life. Thank you for all the good times, all the bad times. Without them I wouldn't be who I am.

Who am I thanking? Life, my higher self, my guides, whoever's listening. I don't think we have to do it all on our own. Somebody's listening.

Sometimes things have happened that have broken my heart. But instead of whimpering, I should've said "THANK YOU!!!" It brought me here, now.

My musings halted as Jeff opened his eyes and smiled at me.

"So you're who my Sunday mornings were waiting for," I whispered.

He laughed. "I missed you when you weren't there yet." I smiled.

"You seem happy with your lot in life," he whispered.

"I have a lot in life."

It was his turn to smile. "All of a sudden there you were and that was that. It's like, of course—that's who I was waiting for."

And he was worth the wait.

We fell back to sleep. In a misty dream, I said to her, "You're my shero, Cyn."

She answered, "You're my shero, Trish." Then she added, "But play a bigger game."

That woke me up. Jeff was in the bathroom. "Yeah, I'm getting on that, Cyn," I said to the air. Correction: I said it to her.

Cyn is still the shero of her journey. She left such an impact. It makes me think of all the people who touched me and of the ones I've touched, perhaps. My family, my friends, my teachers, my industry peeps, my clients... each and every one of us touch and are touched by so many. We all leave particular brushmarks on each other that only we can leave.

I want her back every day of my life; I want us laughing and joking again. I'll even take her macabre moments. I'd change the tightly wound relationship we had so it'd let other people in to have a partnership with, but I want her back. I always will.

Maybe *she* didn't kill herself—maybe her haze of alcohol and pills killed her. Yet, people die. That's what they do. It's not a failure. It's the next step.

And...what if she *wasn't* in a haze in that particular moment in time? What if it was the clearest moment she'd ever had?

I have to respect her decision, her journey, as the master of her soul's journey. Maybe the decision was not at the earthly level, but it was certainly at the soul level.

And she could never kill her *self*, anyway. Death is just a new beginning. Somewhere. Cyndi's continuing there.

Meanwhile, I'm continuing here. Making it medium is kind of cool—and that's what's so far, anyway. Maybe I'll make a great old broad lighting up some movie sometime, swearing and shaking my cane and making people laugh at the Oscars and say, "She makes growing old look so fun." If I make it that long, that is. If I don't, that's fine, too. We can't do it wrong.

This one's a wrap.

IN LOVING MEMORY

of all those
who died trying

CREDITS

My beautiful Steve, who reminds me every day how to live life to the fullest and to follow my dreams, and who keeps me laughing—a lot...as in a lotta lot.

Sherry Robb, thank you for being my friend and literary agent all these years as well as my colleague for that very special time in LA—definitely one of the most fun adventures of my life.

All of the actors I worked with in LA, I love and admire you more than you know. My special LA friends Alpa, Angela, Ariyana, Armand, Billy, Brynda, Carolyn, Connie, Dan, David, Dev, Frank, George, Greg, Hal, Jeffrey, Jennifer, Katt, Klemen, Lisa, Monica, Omid, Roberta, Sheldon, Susan, Suzan, Theo, and Valerie.

Thanks and ginormous hugs to my special team: Athena McDowell, Jenni Ashanta Lipari, Barbara Cox, my sister Betsey Crawford, Dana Swift, Eugene Holden, Jim Self and Roxanne Burnett and the MA Players, Joan and John Walker, Karri Horner-Anderson, Rev. Karyl Huntley, Laurie Manley, Lavandar, Linda Eisenberg, Rev. Dr. Michael Beckwith, and Veronica Entwistle. And because I'll love you forever and beyond, thank you Anjee, Barb, Deb, Grace, Guy, Janet, Rev. Katherine, Kiara, Kim, Rev. Lee, Liz, Samantha, Sue, and Will.

My favorite book-cover designer and dear friend Alysa Sanzari-Hall of SHG Design.

Park Peters, my amazing audio engineer and one of the most light-filled, upbeat people I've ever met.

Barry Goldstein, whose beautiful music provided the soundtrack for writing this book.

Very special thanks to Diane Bishop, Frances Mary Frane, and Kate Hagerty as well as the wonderful women of MyWordPublishing.com, especially Polly Letofsky and Susie Schaefer, and Mary Walewski of buythebookmarketing.com.

My indomitable improv team—Bill, Emma, Jake, Jason, Jo, Kathy, Mitch, Randy, Tama, and TC...and a special shout-out to my/our teachers and coaches Allison, Asa, Heather, Jon, Nick, Misti, and Steve.

A very heartfelt thank you for your words and experiences to Alexander Lehr, Ann Ten Eyck, Rev. Barbara Leger, Cheryl McCoy, Dr. Donese Worden, Doreen Cumberford, Jacob Landis-Eigsti, Karen Daniels, Karen Drucker, Kathleen McGowan, Kayla Gold, Lisa Nichols, Mary Gaul and Liel Lowndes, Melissa Phillippe, Robert McKee, Sandy Handsher, and Sara Davidson. All of the actors, moviemakers, screenwriters, singers, and songwriters referred to in this book and who have immeasurably added their magic to my life and the lives of so, so many.

To the late Fred Blais and the Croton Shakespeare Festival for giving my entire family such a glorious gift for so many years.

My family, with special recognition to my brother Perry, who has a terminal illness. In addition to being the best big brother ever, he gave me my first love of theater at a very young age.

To my friends who have committed suicide: I look forward to the time and place where I get to see you again. I love you so much, and I honor your courage, your decision, and your journey.

Most especially to Nadia Wit and the late Debra Mayer— words cannot convey how much you both mean to me.

BOOKS BY ANN CRAWFORD

Available on Amazon
in paperback, Kindle, and audiobook versions

Fresh off the Starship

Life in the Hollywood Lane

Spellweaver

Angels on Overtime

Mary's Message—
The Story of Mary Magdalene and Yeshua Ben Yosef

Visioning—Creating the Life of Our Dreams
and a World that Works for Us All

ABOUT THE AUTHOR

Ann Crawford's wild-and-crazy background includes being a best-selling author of ten books, a screenwriter, and an award-winning filmmaker. In addition to being on an improv team and doing the odd acting gig here and there, she had a stint in talent management.

After spending most of her adult life in California, she and her family live in Colorado. She has many relatives in Wisconsin—the home state of the book's shero—and has spent a considerable amount of time there. She's also traveled the world extensively: seventy countries and counting as well as all fifty states.

You are welcome to follow Ann's effervescent blog at anncrawford.net as well as visit her on Facebook, Twitter, Instagram, Pinterest, and Amazon—hashtags #AnnCrawfordAuthor and #LoveLightandLaughter.

To inquire about having Ann speak or do a book reading for your group or book club either in person or via Skype, please email info@lightscapespublishing.com.